"O ye of little faith."

"Good morning, Mr. O'Rourke." The swish of skirts behind him spun Brian around. Alice stood smiling, round blue eyes compassionate, one lace-mitted hand extended. He briefly pressed it but couldn't help glancing over her shoulder to the brown-haired, yellow-clad figure behind her.

"Miss Heather?" He looked deep into her eyes. Hopes and dreams died. He saw a flicker that betrayed doubt, if not condemnation, mixed with a look of appeal that rocked him.

"Mr. O'Rourke." Her lifeless greeting confirmed what he read in her gaze and sent him out of the church as soon as he could leave without seeming discourteous.

COLLEEN L. REECE is a prolific author with over eighty books published, including ten **Heartsong Presents** titles. With the popular *Storm Clouds over Chantel*, Reece established herself as a doyenne of Christian romance.

Books by Colleen L. Reece

HEARTSONG PRESENTS
HP1—A Torch for Trinity
HP2—Wildflower Harvest
HP7—Candleshine
HP8—Desert Rose
HP16—Silence in the Sage (with Gary Dale)
HP24—Whispers in the Wilderness (with Gary Dale)
HP43—Veiled Joy
HP52—Tapestry of Tamar
HP64—Crows'-nests and Mirrors (with Albert B. Towne)
HP75—Music in the Mountains (with Gary Dale)

PRESENT TENSE—TWO BOOKS IN ONE
PT1—Interrupted Flight & Delayed Dream

WESTERN COLLECTION—TWO BOOKS IN ONE
WC1—Voices in the Desert & Echoes in the Valley

Flower of Seattle

Colleen L. Reece

Flower Chronicles: Book 1

Heartsong Presents

A note from the author:
I love to hear from my readers! You may correspond with me by writing:

Colleen L. Reece
Author Relations
P.O. Box 719
Uhrichsville, OH 44683

ISBN 1-55748-583-6
FLOWER OF SEATTLE

PRINTED IN THE U.S.A.

prologue

Fifteen-year-old Brian O'Rourke folded his lanky legs and arms like a closed jackknife and hoped the loud beat of his heart wouldn't give him away. If he could remain hidden until the *Cutlass* sailed, he'd be safe. He forced himself to take deep, silent breaths until the thumping in his chest slowed. Muffled shouts, the creaking of timbers and rattle of chains lifted his spirits. *There's no reason for anyone to look under the lifeboat*, he told himself. Yet each time heavy steps came near, another spurt of fear rose within.

An eternity later, the roll and pitch of the sailing ship lulled him into an uneasy sleep. Troublesome dreams tormented him, then settled into memories: his mother, trying to stretch the bit of money Da brought home from long hours of grueling work when he could find any; dim recollections of his early childhood before the potato famine came. Born in 1840, Brian well remembered the great roasts of beef, mutton and pork; the bread and chicken and always potatoes. Then, hunger. Even in his sleep, his belly twisted. The rich Irish stews, the salt pork and cabbage and potatoes had dwindled to thin soups, barely enough to keep body and soul together. Patrick O'Rourke's dark face grew grimmer as 1847 limped in. "'Tis a dark day for us," he often said. Yet all through the unbelievable hardship, the helplessness that eventually took both his and his wife's lives along with 750,000 Irish who died of starvation and disease, the O'Rourkes clung to one thing— pride of country.

"Brian Boru," Patrick told his son. "You carry the name of the greatest Irish king. Never forget that in 1014, High King Brian organized princes and defeated the Vikings. *Erin go bragh, boyeen.*"

"Ireland forever, boy," the huddled figure murmured. The sound of his own voice brought him awake and fearful. Had anyone heard? He held his breath until the freckles that matched his flaming hair threatened to pop off his pale skin but no rough voice ordered him out from under the lifeboat, no cruel hands yanked him into view.

The chain of thought started by his dream clutched him. How long ago it seemed, the happy time followed by days of misery! Somehow Da had scraped up enough to send his only son to a distant relative who saw in the wiry boy cheap labor at only the cost of enough food to keep Brian working twelve, fourteen, sometimes sixteen hours a day with his sheep. The miserly man's promises to send aid to the O'Rourkes proved a goad to the homesick eight-year-old. He endured the squalid corner of the barn assigned to him, forced down his portions of food, and learned to hate the man and his family who wore good clothes and rode in a carriage while Ireland suffered.

More than two years passed. Brian doggedly kept on with his work, even when letters from home ceased and fear thrust red-hot fingers into his mind. So much sickness! Had his parents died? By April 1st, his tenth birthday, Brian knew he must find out. He also knew it was useless to ask his employer. The man turned questions aside. Yet a keen brain lay behind the lake-blue eyes of the boy and his thatch of curly red hair hid his thoughts. That night he slipped away in the darkest early morning hours and started the long journey back.

It took days. A dozen times he thought he'd never make it. A dozen times he asked God for help, the God he'd been taught listened to even a boy's prayers. It came in many ways: a glistening lake or a stream when he needed water, the gift of a bit of food by kindly folk who could ill afford to give it. He slept in deserted huts when he could find them and under trees. Sometimes he wondered if those whose home he had fled had sent word ahead. Would he be caught and sent to gaol? Or back?

"Never!" he told the green hills and valleys. "I am Brian Boru O'Rourke. I have done a man's job." The thought cheered him. Surely he could find a place, one that would offer a meager wage which was more than he'd been given. Times were not quite so hard. Yet the farther he went, the more he wondered what he'd find. New fears assailed him at the news that hundreds of thousands who survived the famine had left their homeland. Surely Da and Mother would never have gone from Ireland, leaving their son behind!

At last he reached his destination, the thatched cottage a few miles from Cork. The door sagged open. Emerald grass and thistles grew between the neat stones that made a path to the door. The lad drew in a hurting, quivering breath and stepped inside. Dust lay thick on the few remaining pieces of hand hewn furniture.

A busy spider swung to safety when Brian brushed the web away from his face. "Mother? Da?"

A slight sound from the doorway terrified him. He whirled.

"Gone. All gone." A crone leaned on a stick, her face gaunt.

"Where?" It burst from his tight throat.

She silently pointed to a gentle rise of land to her left.

Brian stumbled past her and unsteadily walked the short distance. A gentle breeze cooled his face, warm from the sunny day and his long journey. He climbed, came to a level spot of land tucked in the rolling hillocks. Two crude crosses told the story, dated a few days apart and about the time Brian's letters ceased.

"Why, God?" He fell to the earth between the mounds already greening with new grass. "Why?" No answer came. Exhausted by grief, the strength that had kept him going deserted him. Tears gushed, enough to swell the river Shannon. After a long time, Brian slept.

He awakened to the touch of a gnarled hand on his shoulder. Somehow the old woman had managed to climb the hill. "Come, *boyeen*."

Too bewildered to argue, he let her lead him away—past the remains of his home to a tiny hut not far away. Something bubbled in a pot. A bit of a loaf rested on a small table. The wizened woman motioned him to sit on a cot. She brought water and bathed his tear-stained face as she would a small child's. Not until he ate all she brought him did Brian realize she had given him her own supper. He opened his mouth to thank her but surprisingly, her eyes twinkled.

"'Tis glad enough I am for comp'ny. Ye be Brian Boru."

He started at her knowledge but nodded.

"Yer blessed mither said ye'd come." She reached beneath her worn shawl and took out a folded paper. "I niver thought 'twould be so soon but the Good Fither saw to it. Me son's for coming afther me t'morrow."

Brian set his lips at her mention of the Heavenly Father but eagerly took the paper from her hand. The spidery writing little resembled the firm strokes on the letters he once received. They spoke of the weakness in the fingers that made them.

> *Dear Brian Boru,*
> *Da's gone home to our Father and I'll*
> *be with him soon. I'm only sorry I won't*
> *be for seeing you again 'til we meet in*
> *heaven. Always remember how much our*
> *Father loves us and don't grow weary*
> *trying to figure His ways. Da and I'll be*
> *waiting for you. . .*

The last few words were barely legible. Young as he was, Brian understood the great effort his mother had put into leaving him a final message.

He visited the graves once more before leaving. The good-hearted neighbor's son gladly gave the desolate boy a ride into Cork and insisted the boy stay with his family for a time. Too numb to make other plans, Brian accepted but the too-familiar signs of want soon roused his independence. He must not take food from the mouths of the little ones by staying. For the second time he slipped away in the night, but this time with a note telling them he would write someday and let them know where he was.

The next five years passed day by dogged day. Brian grew tall. He gladly accepted whatever job fell to his lot. In spite of his lean build, those for whom he worked discovered he gave more than most men when it came to a day's work. Yet no matter how hard he tried, the boy couldn't put aside any money. Ireland had not recovered from the famine. Perhaps it never would. Now and then the wanderer heard glowing reports from those who had somehow managed to leave Ireland, especially from families who emigrated to America. The very word sent a thrill through the boy. He fingered the page his mother had left, his only inheritance, until it lay in shreds and at last disintegrated. The message had burned into his heart and soul even though he still didn't understand it all. Neither did he understand how a God who supposedly loved him seemed so far away and uncaring. Yet in spite of his struggles, Brian continued to pray—usually that somehow God would help him get to America. Five years almost to the day he'd left his distant relatives, the stripling lad who now stood at almost 5'10" told God, "You haven't helped me. I'll be for doing it myself."

For days he lounged on the docks, blue eyes shaded by an old cap, ears wide open and listening. He knew which ships were scheduled to sail for America and when. He drank in everything he could overhear about the ship captains and crews. Then the night before the *Cutlass* sailed, he crept aboard, his only possessions the ragged clothing he wore and the gnawing desire to

get away from the British Isles. The ship offered few
readily discernible hiding places and Brian dared not
take the risk of detection by prowling, so he carefully
slid under the lifeboat, wondering what lay ahead.
Captains had been known to throw stowaways overboard, according to seafaring tales. The boy's sole hope
lay in Captain Haines, reported to be one of the strict-
est yet fairest men ever to captain a ship. If Brian
could convince Haines to let him work for his passage,
someday he would reach America.

Now he lay in his cramped position, stomach empty
but unwilling to expose himself until he absolutely
couldn't bear the hunger. For three days he managed,
stealing out at night and finding water, but too frightened to seek out the galley and food. "Brian Boru is
no thief," he told his complaining belly. "I will be
able to tell Captain Haines that." He clung to the
thought until it became a talisman, something to sus-
tain him when he knew he couldn't hold out much
longer.

On the fourth day his frail security shattered. The
Cutlass had run into bad weather and the ship's tossing proved too much for the empty stomach. As hard
as he tried not to, Brian heaved and moaned. A heartbeat later, powerful hands flung the lifeboat aside and
jerked the boy to his feet. Brian caught sight of a stern-
faced man he recognized as the Captain and even while
heaving again, a tiny voice in his heart whispered thanks
to God for it being the Captain who discovered him.

"A stowaway! By all the powers of earth and heaven,
a stowaway on my ship." The massive Captain glared
at the hapless Brian. "Thought you could get away

with it, didn't you?" He shook the culprit as a wolf shakes a captured rabbit.

Without stopping to consider, Brian's free right hand snapped to his forehead in a salute. "Brian Boru O'Rourke reporting for duty, sir."

In the frozen moment that followed, he saw the Captain's jaw drop open, then heard his roar. "Of all the—you'll come with me, O'Rourke." His ham-hand fastened even tighter on the stowaway's ragged shirt and he propelled Brian ahead of him until they reached the Captain's cabin, hurled him inside, then demanded, "Give me one good reason I shouldn't drop you overboard." He crossed his arms and his chest swelled. His graying blond hair strayed from beneath his cap and his steely gaze never left the offender's face. "Stowing away, sneaking out nights and stealing food—"

"I have taken nothing except water." Brian swallowed hard to keep the bile from overflowing again. "I am no thief." His lip curled. "The O'Rourkes work for their keep."

"Work! What need have I of a skinny kid like you? How old are you? Do your parents know where you are? For the love of the saints, why did you stow away aboard the *Cutlass* instead of some other ship?"

The fusillade of questions hit Brian like grapeshot. With what little dignity he could muster he squared his shoulders, rose and stood before his judge and jury. "I've worked hard since I turned eight. I'm fifteen. My parents are both dead." He paused, saw a flicker of something unreadable in the Captain's face, and took a deep breath. "Sure, Captain Haines, and you'd have done the same thing if you were me."

For a moment while his fate hung in the balance, Brian suspected he'd gone too far. The next instant, Captain Haines let out a shout of laughter that shook Brian even more than his earlier roaring had done. He caught the boy's hand in a grip that left Brian's hand tingling and started a fire of hope in his heart. "You're right about that, you Irish scamp," he bellowed. "Ever worked on a ship?"

"No, but I can learn." He put his last remaining strength into his handclasp and felt rewarded by Haines' grin. Although his head roared, he managed to say, "If I could have some water, I'll be able to show you."

"Are you telling the truth about not stealing food?"

"I am."

Captain Haines raised his voice and called but Brian didn't hear what he said, too caught up in trying not to heave again. He managed and when Haines pushed him to a chair he fell into it. Someone shoved a bowl of heavenly-smelling stew in front of him and Haines ordered, "Eat, but not too fast."

Every bite of the rich broth, and chunks of meat and vegetables brought renewed strength. At last Brian laid down his spoon. "Thank you, sir. I'll be taking orders now."

Haines' glare nailed him to his seat. "Not so fast, Irishman. We'll just have us a little talk first." At his insistence, Brian frankly gave his whole story. He ended with, "I had to get away. I heard you were strict and fair and hoped you'd be for giving me a chance."

The Captain threw his hands in the air. "What part of Ireland do you come from?"

"Near Cork."

"Ever been to Blarney Castle?"

The question caught Brian off guard. "Why, yes." A fugitive grin that hadn't seen the light of day for months blossomed. "That's where the Blarney Stone is."

The Captain looked skyward as if imploring divine help. "It figures. You must have kissed it, what with your convincing me not to feed you to the fish." He considered for a time, pacing the narrow area. "All right, Blarney O'Rourke. I'll give you a chance. It means working like you've never worked before. If you'll do everything I say—and you'll answer to me and no other man on the *Cutlass*—you can earn passage to America. The food's plain and your quarters will be with the paying passengers, the lowest of them, of course."

Brian bit his lip. Only too well did he know how terrible conditions were on many ships, especially for the poor people who barely scraped up money enough to buy fare.

Captains Haines raised a sandy eyebrow. "This is no coffin boat. We ain't fancy but I don't aim to have any more burials at sea than what can't be avoided." He eyed the boy's ragged clothing and the corners of his mouth turned down. "See the quartermaster and tell him to outfit you and throw those rags overboard. We'll have no vermin aboard my ship."

Brian's head snapped back. "I carry no vermin, Captain. And I washed my clothes the day before I—uh—reported for duty."

Another bellow of laughter greeted him and a prayer of thankfulness went up from the new sailor's heart. He threw himself into the work given him and took his turn at everything from swabbing the deck to peeling vegetables for the taciturn cook. Captain Haines had put the word out O'Rourke was to be left strictly alone; what discipline he needed would be meted out by the Captain only. Brian knew that but for Haines' order he would have been subjected to all the horrors that accompanied stowing away.

The plain food, hard work, and sea air did their task well. For the first time since early childhood, Brian went to bed with his belly full. His tall frame began to fill out and by the time the voyage ended, he looked more man than boy. The morning the ship docked, Captain Haines called him aside.

"O'Rourke, how bent are you on staying in America?"

Brian stared. "Why, it's all I've thought and dreamed of."

Haines gazed at him with piercing eyes, softened to the gray of Atlantic fog. "Lad, you're a good sailor. If you want a place aboard the *Cutlass*, it's yours. We'll be sailing in a week." His eyed glistened. "Stick with me and you'll see the seven seas and a lot more." He cleared his throat. "You don't have to answer now."

Brian looked at the man who had in some measure replaced Da. He thought of the exhilaration of trying to outrace a storm, the sunrises and sunsets that left him speechless, most of all, the big man before him. He turned to glance at the shore. America, place of opportunity. Never had he felt more torn. In order to birth a new dream, the old must die.

"It won't be forever, lad." Captain Haines smiled. "I figure I'm good for maybe ten years more. You'll still be a young man and one with a pouch. I've noticed how you refuse the drink and games of chance. Wouldn't it be better to face life in a new land with money in your belt?" He threw up his hands. "There, Blarney, if I'm not trying to convince you when I've just said you need not decide now! Well, I'll keep my word."

With a look of relinquishment, Brian squared his shoulders as he had done months earlier and snapped a salute. "Brian Boru O'Rourke reporting for duty, sir." He found his reward in the searching eyes and the grip of his Captain's big hand.

Captain Haines proved to be as good a predictor of the future as he was a weather prophet. Just under ten years later, he died at sea, a short distance off the coast of California. Brian could not grieve too much. He'd seen the powerful man cringe as he grew weaker from a faulty heart that couldn't be repaired. Once Haines confessed, "The idea of living out my last days on land leaves me shaking. A sailor needs the sea."

A few days later he simply didn't wake up and Brian rejoiced. In the final weeks Haines had turned even more to the worn Bible and made his peace with his Maker.

"At first it seemed a kind of scurvy trick to come to Him when the final storm hovered," he told Brian, long since called Blarney by the *Cutlass* crew. "Then I read John 3:16 again and again. 'For God so loved the world that, He gave His only begotten Son, that whosoever believeth in Him should not perish, but have everlasting life.' It doesn't say anything about it having to be when a man's young. I reckon that word *whosoever* means an old salt like me, too."

Searching his memories for long-forgotten gems, Brian nodded. "That's what Da always said."

"Lad." The Captain reverted to the simple appellation he used only in the most poignant moments. "I'd like to think we'll meet again, but there's only one Way."

"I'm for knowing that, sir."

"Don't wait like I did. I had a good life. The sea's been friend, wife, family. I'm only sorry my life didn't count more for Him." He gruffly added, "I've not much to leave. The *Cutlass* isn't mine. But what I do have is yours." He rested his hand on the Bible. "Including this. It's the best thing I can do for you."

Brian couldn't answer.

Presently Haines continued. "What will you do? Stay with the ship."

"No. Not without you." He didn't explain that for the past two years a restlessness had overcome his love of the sea, a desire to be a landlubber at least for a time.

"You won't go back to Ireland." Certainty underscored the words. "Blarney, I hear there's excitement aplenty in Washington Territory. Seattle's said to be greener than anything this side of Ireland. A man who gets in on the making of a city—and you'll have a stake—might do well."

Brian remembered his Captain's words. The day after the *Cutlass* docked, he bade farewell to his mates and headed north.

one

Puget Sound and the forests surrounding Seattle brought an involuntary, "Sure, and if a body were to settle, it'd be here" from Brian O'Rourke when he first arrived early in 1865. "Captain Haines said it right. It's for being almost as green as Ireland."

The years at sea had added muscle. At twenty-five, his blue eyes remained bright as ever. So did his flaming hair, although his freckles had faded. He stood a proud 5'10" and weighed in at 170 pounds of catlike grace and the strength of a modern Samson. Within hours of reaching Seattle, he found work in the woods. Before long, he could pull a saw or make chips fly with the most seasoned logger. The older hands grudgingly showed respect for the way he took to the work. The younger crew members also respected him, chiefly for his flying, deadly fists.

One old-timer drawled, "You'd never think that cocky grin of his could change so fast when there's an underdog to be defended. Why, I thought he'd break Miller in two for mopping up the floor with that green kid who couldn't do anything but take it!"

"Yeah," another agreed. "Funny thing. He joshes and gets along with 'most everyone. I've seen him laugh when the rest of us would come out swingin'. But just let a feller look crosswise at someone who ain't a fighter, and good-bye Hannah!"

When Brian overheard "Blarney O'Rourke's feats" being discussed he grinned to himself and his eyes sparkled with fun. Even to himself, he couldn't say why something in him demanded that he stick up for the more helpless. He suspected it had something to do with Captain Haines regretting his own life hadn't counted more for God. Now and then Brian dipped into the old Bible. He fastened onto the verse, *And the king shall answer and say unto them, Verily I say unto you, Inasmuch as ye have done it unto one of the least of these my brethren, ye have done it unto me.** Until the time came when he could resolve his mixed feelings about God and Jesus, he'd try to help a few along the way who needed his fighting Irish skills.

Early one spring evening, his day's work done, Brian plunged into a faint trail not far from camp. The many shades of green rested his eyes: hemlock and cedar, fir and spruce; giant sword ferns, the green of bracken. A lone eagle sailed overhead. Squirrels scolded and bluejays raucously blended their cries with the sweeter bird song of robins and little birds the meandering logger didn't recognize. A touch of the rolling gait acquired by trodding heaving decks remained in his walk. He liked his fellow loggers but something within cried out for solitude now and then, a time to be away from the laughter and cards, inevitable arguing and loose talk. Brian had never seen himself as a loner, yet he hadn't grown close to any man since Captain Haines died. He also avoided entanglements with women. Always courteous to the hardy loggers' wives who courageously made homes in the wilderness for their men, he refused to degrade himself as some of his

*Matthew 25:40

companions did on their trips into Seattle. Their boasting of conquests made him soul-sick.

Now he sat on a huge stump left from cutting, a good four feet across the butt. "Wish I'd had a brother. I guess I'm a bit lonely." His confession sounded loud in the quiet forest. From habit he took the Bible from his shirt where he'd placed it before starting out. He also made sure the rifle he carried leaned near. Bears and cougars abounded in the woods. They usually shied away from the loggers but no man ever left camp without a rifle.

Brian read until slanting shadow warned dusk would overtake him before he got back to camp unless he started immediately. He stood, stretched and picked up his rifle, at peace with himself and the forest that surrounded him.

He hadn't realized how far he'd come. Only a glimmer of light remained when he reached the final fork in the little-used trail. He speeded up. Just around the bend he'd be able to see the lights of camp. His stomach grumbled and he thought of the bowl of apples the cook left set out for hardworking men who wanted something between their prodigious supper and breakfast meals.

Head back, gaze straight ahead, Brian didn't notice the obstruction in the path until the toe of his boot caught on something. He tried to right himself but the momentum from his rapid stride sent him plunging forward and down. His rifle fell to the ground. His outstretched hands touched the inert form beneath him. He recoiled, leaped to his feet, and backed off a step from sheer horror. He shook his head and squinted, hoping against hope he'd find himself waking from a nightmare.

His hope faded with the last of the light. A body lay crumpled in the path, one hand pitifully outstretched in a mute appeal for help.

"God, is he dead?" Brian knelt, groped until he felt a belt buckle, then moved his hand upwards and laid his ear over a rough-jacketed chest. A faint, distant thunderlike beating brought a sigh of relief and Brian's callused hands sought for what had felled the man. When he touched the head, his hand came away warm and sticky.

A furtive movement from the side of the trail alerted him. Had the attacker come to finish his job? Brian felt for and found his rifle, cocked it in one motion and called, "Come out with your hands up or I'll be for shooting."

A curse and the thrashing of undergrowth answered him. Brian raised the rifle toward the sky and shot. Not unless his life or the victim's depended on it would he kill. Another curse and pounding footsteps sounded, farther away. Brian fired again. Waited. Fired a third shot. "You dirty skunk," he cried.

"Is that you, Blarney?" The sound of men running from the direction of camp drowned out the retreating steps.

"Here. Someone's bad hurt." He recognized the straw boss's voice when the man shouted, "Bring a lantern. And a stretcher." Dark shapes burst around the bend in the trail. A lantern bobbed and grew brighter. Angry loggers muttered and crowded close.

"Hold the light down so we can see. Aw, it's a kid."

A string of curses profaned the air.

Brian looked at the pallid face of a boy hardly out of his teens, ghastly-looking in the steady glow of lantern light. "I don't think he has any broken bones," he ventured.

The straw boss nodded. "Good, but I'll be a spotted dog if he ain't got a skull fracture. Move him real careful-like."

The Irishman marveled as he had so many times before at the incredible gentleness of the rough loggers with a hurt or wounded comrade. They got him to the bunkhouse, undressed him and stood back muttering while the straw boss, who had a rude understanding of medical knowledge, examined him, then barked, "Miller, drive to town and get a doctor. Make him come if you have to shoot him in the leg. This boy's hurt bad."

The big logger, who surprisingly had never held it against Brian for interfering in his harassing the kid, leaped for the door. "Right, boss." He slammed out and in an incredibly short time the sound of wagon wheels on the skid road echoed and died.

Hours later Miller and the doctor arrived, a grave-faced man whose countenance grew stern when he examined the boy. "Lost a lot of blood. Skull fracture, probably, but doesn't seem to be any displacement of bones. Best thing for him is rest and what food you can get into him. How much blood did he lose? How long before someone found him?"

"I don't know," Brian admitted. "I'd say not too long. The jasper who did this either heard me coming or was on his way back to finish the job."

"Anything on him to show who he is?" the doctor barked.

"No. His pockets were empty." The straw boss shot a significant glance at the doctor who shook his head in disgust.

"There's a lot of yay-hoos around with mighty taking ways," he snorted. His quick glance around the circle of watching men sent a chill down Brian's spine. Surely the doctor didn't think—

"You sayin' it was one of us?" Miller bulled his way to the doctor, face black with anger. "We ain't no Sunday school saints but we don't strike down our own and steal from them."

A murmur of assent swept through the bunkhouse and Brian relaxed. The thought of being part of a group that housed a killer made him sick.

"So who's gonna play nurse?" Miller wanted to know.

"I will if I can be spared," Brian volunteered. "You can dock my pay, if you like."

"Huh, like to see anyone try." The straw boss grinned and his eyes gleamed. "I reckon since he shouldn't be moved, the kid's our responsibility. Doc, you'll be out again?"

"Soon as I can." A long sigh escaped. "We could use a dozen doctors and three times that many nurses in this cussed land. Never saw such a place for folks getting hurt and sick." He complained all the way out but Brian sensed every man present knew that beneath the gruff exterior lay a dedicated physician.

Miller confirmed it by saying, "Grumpy old sawbones but none better. If any of you fellers pound my noggin 'til I need a doc, fetch him."

Late the next morning, long after all the men except Brian had gone into the woods and the cook and his helpers busied themselves in the cook shack, the white-faced boy opened hazel eyes, licked his lips, and tried to speak.

"Don't talk," Brian warned. "You're at the logging camp. I found you hurt on the trail. Here, drink this." He fetched cool water and gently raised the tousled brown head until the patient could eagerly drink. A little later the boy's eyes cleared of fuzziness and his nurse brought rich broth. By the time the men swarmed in, sweaty and laughing, Brian had given in and propped pillows up behind the bandaged head. Yet they didn't get the story until after supper. Brian had eaten early and carried a plate of steaming potatoes, gravy, meat and vegetables back to the bunkhouse. It vanished like mist over Puget Sound flees before the sunlight.

"Now, young feller." The straw boss parked himself on a chair drawn up next to the patient while the others lounged on their bunks, in the open doorway, and just outside where they could hear from the long, covered porch. "Want to tell us what happened? Who are you, anyway, and what're you doing here? How old are you?"

"Twenty." A ripple of surprise ran through the listening ranks. A wan smile crossed the boy's face. "I know. I don't look it but I am. I mean I will be, June first. I've been in Seattle for almost three years, working on the docks and in stores." His smile disappeared. "Haven't been able to save fast enough to bring my sweetheart out, even though she's wild to come."

A thrill went through Brian. What must it be like to

have a sweetheart, a girl who could bring such a tender look to a man's face?

"My name's Harry Templeton." He restlessly moved his head and grimaced. Exploring fingers gingerly touched the bandage and an expression of pain crossed his face. "I heard you needed men and paid good wages. Got a ride part way with a man who's built a cabin in a clearing not far away but it grew dusky before I could get here." He wrinkled his forehead. "I can't remember anything except thinking I'd take a shortcut the settler talked about."

"We wondered about that," Miller interrupted. "No one 'cept Blarney ever walks on that old game trail." The other men laughed at his wit.

"Blarney? I though he said his name was Brian."

"Sure, and he's for bein' an Irishman and the son of an Irishman," Miller mimicked in an atrocious Irish accent. "Niver saw such a one for talkin' the birds out of the trees."

When they settled down again Harry continued. "I though I heard something alongside the trail. Didn't know but what it might be a wild animal so I walked faster. The next thing I knew I woke up and Br-Blarney told me not to talk."

"There's something mighty fishy about this," Miller bluntly said. "We know it wasn't none of us. We ain't mean and we ain't thieves." He puckered his face into a fearsome sight. "Boss, I reckon we better pay a leetle visit to that settler. Templeton, did you happen to mention you were savin' to send for your girl?"

"Why, yes. But I don't carry the money with me."

"Did he know that?" Miller relentlessly questioned.

"No." Harry admitted, hazel eyes beginning to show understanding.

"What did he get from you, if you don't mind my asking?" the straw boss put it.

"Coupla dollars I carry for jingle."

Miller walked to the door, black anger in his face. "And he almost killed you for that! Come on, boys. We're gonna catch ourselves a murderin' varmint." A stampede followed.

"You stay," the straw boss ordered Brian. "I'll just see the settler gets hauled to town and jail." He gave a sour grin. "I don't want the boys getting carried away with justice and holding a necktie party with the settler as guest of honor."

"I don't want anyone to get hung on account of me," Harry Templeton told Brian when the others had gone. "A few dollars isn't worth a life. Besides, we aren't positive he did it." His faithful attendant agreed but they both changed their minds when the disgruntled crew returned.

"Feller has cleared out. Cabin ain't finished and no sign of crops. Looks to us like he weren't no settler a-tall," Miller said. "Wonder how far he'll get on your money? 'Course, he could be one of them slick gamblers or someone hidin' out. Anyway, he's gone. Anyone want a cabin? It's shore in a pretty spot." He grinned at Harry. "Say, the way I figure, the cabin's yours, bought and paid for. Think that gal of yours would like living in the woods with a bunch of no-good loggers for neighbors?"

A thoughtful look crept into the clear, hazel eyes under the thatch of light brown hair. "Alice said she'd

be willing to live anywhere to be with me," he told
them. "If I finished the cabin, it would mean I wouldn't
need as much money to get a house and she could come
a lot quicker. You really think I can lay claim to it?"

"I'll check on it in town the next time I'm in," the
straw boss promised. "Now, let's get some shut-eye.
Morning comes mighty early."

Long after the even breathing mingled with snores
and proclaimed the men slept, Brian lay wide awake.
He'd taken a liking to Harry, seeing in the game kid
something of himself in his teens. What if he worked
out a deal where until Alice came, they could fix the
cabin and live together? It would give him privacy and
in turn, he'd help Harry get the cabin ready. The more
he pondered the idea, the better he liked it. Even on
shipboard, he'd never enjoyed living with other men
twenty-four hours a day; as soon as he could, he'd
sought out quarters a bit apart. Now the opportunity
loomed as a godsend. Besides, until Templeton fully
healed—and the doctor said it would take weeks before he regained his energy—Brian could tone down
the boy's eagerness that could result in overtaxing himself.

The next day Harry insisted he was able to look after
himself and proved it by taking a few steps before triumphantly sagging back on his bunk. "I'll holler for
the cook if I need anything. Go on back to work," he
impatiently ordered Brian. A week later the doctor pronounced the boy well on the mend and the camp rejoiced. That evening after supper Brian asked Harry
to take a walk.

"To my cabin?"

"Sure. The boss says it's yours, all legal-like." He didn't add that the men had chipped in and paid a small fee to ensure no one could take the land which it turned out had never been filed on by the bogus settler.

Harry strode along, showing no sign of his injury. He topped Brian by an inch in height, appeared just as strong and had a cheerful attitude toward life that made friends easily. Now he told his new friend and rescuer how he happened to be in Seattle at such an early age. "I had a great family," he said. "Until Mother died five years ago. It did something to Father. Heather, my sister, took care of us. She's a wonder." His face clouded over. "A year later Father remarried, a woman just a few years older than Heather and me." He fell silent and added irrelevantly, "I once read the name Adelaide meant noble and kind. She wasn't." The succinct summarization dismissed the stepmother's attributes. "She goaded Father to push me into the Union Army, using flattery and women's wiles. I refused to fight a war that could only end as it has, with brother against brother, state against state." A bitter cast of his lean face told Brian far more than the words. "I ran away, but not before Alice promised to marry me. Her folks don't know it, only my twin—"

"Twin! You didn't mention him."

"He's a she. Heather and Harry, actually, Harrison Templeton the Second, twins." Regret filled his eyes. "I can't even imagine how hard it must be for Heather. She isn't strong like I am. She's gentle and tries to please. She used to shield me from Father when he got angry. Then it was Adelaide. I miss her almost as much as I do Alice. Twins share something no one

else can. When they're apart, it's like half is missing."
He looked sheepish. "You probably think I'm crazy,
babbling on like this. You wouldn't, if you knew
Heather." Doubt crept across his clearly defined features. "Maybe I should have stuck and protected her,
but when it came to either fighting or fleeing, I left."

"Do you hear from her?" The plight of the unknown
twin sister touched Brian's melted-butter heart.

"A lot. She doesn't complain much but I know she's
unhappy." Harry buttoned his lip and didn't say anything more until they reached the clearing, decided it
could be made into a real home and started back. Then
he said, "There's money involved. Some ancestor left
Father a ton of it. Too bad he wouldn't pass on some
to me when I came out here! Anyway, Adelaide's doing everything she can to turn him away from Heather
as well now that I'm out of it. She's tried to marry her
off ever since I left. Once Heather's driven away,
Adelaide will have every chance of seeing the money
is diverted to her." Worry made him look old for a
moment.

"Sometimes I'm afraid Heather will up and marry
just to escape. I've been over it in my mind until my
brain ached but don't know what I can do. The wind-
fall of getting the cabin and land means I can send for
Alice, maybe by next spring." He hesitated then low-
ered his voice. "I've prayed that God would send a
miracle, something to bring in enough money for
Heather to run away and come to me. She'd always
have a home with Alice and me."

Brian stopped short in the trail. His blue eyes flamed.
His heart pounded. "Harry, I don't know much about

miracles but I'm for being sure things will work out. I have an idea and I want you to listen hard. If you'll let me live in the cabin with you until Alice comes, I'll help you get it ready. I have a pouch of savings, not a lot, but enough for a good start on your sister's passage money. If we work hard all summer and fall, we can spend the winter when the logging camp will be shut down for snow making furniture and the like."

A burst of glory lightened Harry's countenance. A big drop formed and fell unnoticed. "You'd do that— for me?" he choked. "It's more than my own father . . ." He bit off the rest of the sentence and clutched Brian's arm until it ached. "Why? You barely know me."

Brian turned and faced southwest, thinking of a burial at sea. "Ten years ago the Captain of a gallant ship, the *Cutlass*, gave a fifteen-year-old stowaway a chance when that boy stood sick and frightened. I think he'd be happy to know I can pass on his kindness."

"God bless you," Harry cried, then lunged down the trail out of sight, leaving Brian to follow. That night the red-headed sailor-turned-logger dreamed of a strange young woman, whose face was an exact replica of her brother's except for its sweetness. He awakened before dawn, his ears filled with her whisper, "God bless you, Brian Boru O'Rourke" and even the whine of saws and the warning call, "Timber!" could not erase the lingering blessing.

two

Adelaide Templeton turned from the ornate, gilt-framed mirror where she had been preening. Her blond coiffure, far too elaborate for a weekday morning at home, topped a handsome but petulant face. Angry red mottled her clear skin. "What do *you* want?"

Her stepdaughter colored at the rude question. Her sensitive mouth trembled. For a second unexpressed rebellion crept into her soft hazel eyes that went so well with the soft fall of light brown hair.

Before she could answer, Adelaide demanded, "Why is your hair down at this hour? Can't you remember your father wants it in a braid except for evenings?" Her thin lips curved into an unpleasant smile. "I suppose you think having that straight hair hanging down your back makes you look pretty." She laughed harshly, a sound that grated on the girl's nerves. "The only thing pretty about you is your ridiculous name. Heather! Only a heathen would name her child after a bush."

Although past experience had proved the folly of fighting back, Heather Templeton could not let the slur pass. She raised her chin, unexpectedly firm in such a vulnerable face, and retorted, "My mother was the finest Christian I ever knew. She *and Father*—" She stressed the word, "—chose my name to remind them of Scotland." A smile at the memory of her laughing mother spread over her solemn face and a faraway look crept into the eyes shaded by long lashes. "They even brought a bit with them when they came to America." She straightened to her full 5'7" height, a lanky nemesis in a simple blue morning gown. "You can't have forgotten how it flourished until you ordered it removed."

"Hateful stuff." Adelaide stopped her attack long enough to glance out the window. "It still isn't all rooted out but it will be, I promise you that." The venom in her voice hung in the early summer air.

"Why do you hate me so?" Heather burst out, knowing full well she'd pay and pay for it, but pushed so hard she could not remain silent. "First you drove Harry away and now you're trying to do the same with me."

"Any son of a former soldier such as your father who refuses to fight is a sniveling coward and unworthy of the Templeton name."

"Don't you mean the Templeton money?" Heather's hand flew to her mouth and she backed away from the tornado that flew at her, spitting language no lady should use, words whose meaning Heather didn't understand.

Adelaide pursued Heather out the door into the hall and to the top of the stairs, shrieking at the top of her voice.

"You wait until your father hears of this, missy. If you weren't a girl, he'd give you a hiding for being insolent to his wife."

From the safety of halfway down the staircase, Heather flung back in the deadly quiet voice that infuriated her stepmother beyond belief, "If my father were here you wouldn't speak to me in such a manner."

Emboldened by the effect of her words on her adversary, she ran lightly down the hall below but froze when Adelaide screamed, "You mealy-mouthed, white-faced hypocrite! And you call yourself a Christian. Bah." She took a menacing step forward. Her face darkened with rage. "The Bible says children are to honor their fathers and mothers."

An unrepentant grin twitched at Heather's lips. This wasn't the first time the woman had quoted Scripture to make a point. Too heartsick and disgusted with the terrible scene to be cautious, she returned, "Sorry, Adelaide. It says nothing about honoring stepmothers." She wrestled open the heavy front door of the home where she'd been born and went into the garden, forgetting the grocery boy at the back door waiting for the Templeton order. Remorse would come later, she knew. It always did. Retribution from her father also hovered, an ugly black cloud fueled by Adelaide's version of the incident. Try as she would, the memory of her stepmother's hatred couldn't be banished.

Heather wandered aimlessly down paths once made joyous by her mother's feet. The girl's earliest memories centered on cool evenings and warm afternoons in that garden. Mother, in a light gown. Father, face alight with pride in his family. Harry, always the leader in their little games. Now her heart ached. Sometimes she wondered if she'd ever see Harry again. A continent lay between the mansion in New York and the raw new Washington Territory where her twin labored. If only Adelaide had never come into their home and turned it into a house of discontent. Heather sighed.

The year between Mother's death and Adelaide's arrival had been far different from the earlier happy times, yet in spite of his grief, Harrison Templeton spent time with his children. Heather capably directed the servants as she'd been taught to do. Harry studied hard with his tutor, longing for his father's seldom-given approval. Heather's governess at last admitted she could offer the girl no more and departed.

Heather parted the branches of an evergreen that swept the ground like wide skirts at a ball and slipped through. On the other side a patch of heather bloomed. She took a small cluster of bell-shaped purple-rose blossoms and crushed them in her hand, then held them to her hot face. "God, I'm sorry." Her head drooped along with the bruised flowers. "I know You don't want me to answer back but it's so hard, especially when she tries to poison Father against me."

A little breeze sprang up and cooled her burning cheeks. The thought came, *no one will ever poison your Heavenly Father against you,* and comfort stole into her battered heart. It gave her the strength to face her grim parent and triumphant stepmother a few hours later. Harrison had come home for the midday meal and his wife lost no time enumerating Heather's sins. Not one word of her own part in the debacle fell from her thin lips.

"How many times have I told you I won't permit this senseless, unprovoked torturing of your mother?" Harrison slammed the table with a big fist, heedless of the serving maid who scuttled toward the kitchen after a sympathetic glance that told Heather how much the servants would take her part if they dared. The contrast between their treatment by the two mistresses of the Templeton mansion was legendary in the scullery.

Unprovoked! Heather's good intentions fled. "She isn't my mother. She never will be. She hates me and—"

"Silence!" he thundered. "Go to your room and stay there until you can apologize to my wife."

Heather allowed herself one long, reproachful look before standing. Supported by the natural dignity her mother had instilled in her, she walked tall across the enormous dining room and up to her room. Long ago when other children made fun of her for shooting up above them, Heather resorted to walking stooped over and head down. Her wise mother talked with her daughter. "Walk tall, my darling," she had said, her soft brown hair and hazel eyes so like Heather's making a picture in the young girl's heart. "God has created you to stand straight for Him, like a beautiful birch tree. Walk with your head up, shoulders back and look life in the face." Love filled her voice and she embraced Heather. "God allows storms to come but never forget, He's with us always."

A long time later Heather heard footsteps in the hall outside her suite of rooms. She didn't move from the rocker she'd dropped into when she came up. "Quick, Miss, open the door," came a faint whisper.

Heather hastened to obey. "Katie, you shouldn't have done it." She pulled the serving maid who held a covered tray in her hands inside and quickly closed the door.

A stubborn line went around the little maid's mouth. "I won't be caught and if I am, I'll close my ears when the mistress scolds. I heard the master say he'd have no more changing of servants. His eyes are by way of being opened, I think." She removed the cover and exposed roast chicken, potatoes and rich gravy, a dish of sliced ripe tomatoes, another of steaming green beans, and a small plate with a generous wedge of caramel cake. "Ring when you're through. Himself and Her have gone out in the carriage." She hesitated and her honest blue eyes looked straight at Heather. "If you ever need friends, why, there's not a servant here who wouldn't help you, even if it meant giving up our places."

The loyalty in her voice warmed the troubled girl's heart. "Thank you, Katie. I-I'll remember that."

"I have to get back to my job." She awkwardly patted Heather's hand. "Eat every bite." She opened the door. "Say, don't you have a birthday soon?"

"June first."

"Next week." Katie smiled mysteriously and vanished with a swish of crisp uniform and apron.

To her own amazement, Heather did exactly what Katie ordered and enjoyed every bite of her smuggled meal. Once the little maid took away the tray and said goodnight, Heather bathed, slipped into a pale yellow gown and thin negligee, and settled into the rocker. From where she sat, Bible in her lap, she could see out the broad window past blossoming fruit trees to a shining river beyond. Her room faced west and not a day passed that she didn't end by turning toward that window and praying for her twin. It had been some time since she heard from him. If only there were a way for her to get to Washington Territory! Until the scales dropped from Father's eyes, life here would be a continuing series of unpleasant encounters.

Heather recalled the first time she had seen Adelaide, coifed and stylish but unable to hide the aversion to Harrison's children in her hard blue eyes.

"We were married this morning," Harrison had said. "Adelaide is young enough to be your companion and old enough to be my beloved wife."

Heather's stomach knotted the way it had done then. Harry's mouth dropped open and she knew with the uncanny, twinlike way they had of discerning each other's thoughts his mind echoed her own observation—Adelaide wasn't as young as she pretended. Before the first month of her reign ended, the new mistress dropped all pretense of even common courtesy to her stepchildren except in Harrison's presence. Then came the War. It raged no more fiercely than the war between father and son. When Harry could take no more, he clung to his twin, then tore free and walked away without looking back.

If only I could do the same! Heather inwardly cried. God, is there a way? She spent a sleepless night devising a way she could smooth things over yet not lie. So long as she lived in her father's house, his wife deserved a certain respect for position, if not for self. The next morning at breakfast she hesitated outside the dining room and again rehearsed her little speech. Her hands clenched beneath the folds of her pale pink gown and she stepped inside.

"So you finally decided to come down," Adelaide said disagreeably. Sunlight from a window beside her made a halo of her fluffy yellow hair and Heather passed her own place at her father's right, marched to the end of the table and stood beside her stepmother.

"I apologize for yesterday," she quietly said.

Adelaide laid down her silver fork. "You certainly should."

"That's enough," the head of the household told her. "She's said she's sorry."

"She didn't say that at all and I don't believe she's sorry, either," the woman persisted.

"I said that's enough." Harrison Templeton stared coldly at his wife. "We'll hear no more about it."

Adelaide subsided and Heather slipped into her place and forced herself to eat. She didn't dare glance at her stepmother. The hope lighted in her heart by her father's unaccustomed response might show and cause even more trouble. Had Katie been right? Were his eyes being slowly opened to what kind of woman he had chosen to mother his children?

In the days before her birthday, she had reason to believe it might be true. Her father thoughtfully asked her what she'd like. "A party? It's been a long time since you asked your friends in." His forehead wrinkled and she knew he'd just noticed.

"Could we visit Mother's grave and have lunch afterwards?"

He looked jolted but hastily recovered his composure. "Of course. Adelaide can spend time with some of her women friends."

Heather hugged to herself the thought of a half-day with her father. She prayed earnestly some way would open for her to tell him she didn't mean to be hateful. How could she let him know, without criticizing

Adelaide, the position she had been put into for the last year? Or would it simply be better to endure, say nothing and enjoy the rare treat of time alone with the father she devotedly loved in spite of everything?

She needn't have worried. The last day of May when Harrison announced his plans for celebrating his daughter's twentieth birthday, Heather saw hatred more deadly than ever before on her stepmother's face before it adjusted into its usual expression.

"Why, Harrison, I wish you'd told me." Her voice reminded Heather of honey, sticky, and cloying. "I've already arranged a luncheon and afternoon outing for her. A girl only turns twenty once, you know, and most are married by then. You can take her some other time."

Heather knew she lied. The shocked expression had betrayed her. She anxiously looked at her father. Her spirits shot to her toes when she saw the pleased expression on his face. "Why, Adelaide, how kind!" He smiled at Heather. "Of course we can go some other time."

She knew they wouldn't but what could she do? To gain time, she deliberately dropped her napkin on the rich carpet and used the moment of searching to compose herself. "Thank you, Adelaide," she said when she straightened, forcing tranquillity although the older woman's face flamed with victory.

❧

Sometimes life felt like one impossible mountain after another. Even her father's gift of a delicate cameo that had belonged to her mother, and his expression when he said, "It looked like her and you're very much like her, child," didn't help much.

Adelaide immediately put in, "It's lovely, of course,

but doesn't go at all with the pink gown I had Katie press for you. Wear the locket your father and I gave you last Christmas."

Too disappointed to argue, Heather docilely allowed Katie to fasten the tiny buttons on the frilly pink gown and clasp the chain at the nape of her neck. She couldn't resist pulling one long lock of hair, curled for the occasion, over her shoulder until it partially obscured the gaudy trinket she privately detested.

At least the luncheon proved enjoyable. Adelaide had convinced Harrison the half-dozen girls would rather be free of adults and drove away with him in the carriage just before the first arrived.

Alice Freeman, flaxen-haired, with round face and rounder blue eyes, didn't wait to be announced but hurried in and embraced Heather. Her eyes sparkled. "Seeing you is the next best thing to seeing my secret fiancé," she whispered.

"So that's why you come to see me." Heather pretended she'd taken offense. "I thought you were my best friend and here it's just because you miss Harry."

"Don't be a goose." Alice released her. "You look so pretty. Pink is a good color for you. I'm surprised Adelaide allows you to wear it." She didn't wait for an answer but rushed on. "She sure waited until the last minute to invite me to this party. What am I, an afterthought?"

"Not you. The party. I'll explain later," Heather hurriedly told her when the other guests clustered around her, a rainbow of pretty gowns brightening the rather somber room.

The servants had outdone themselves with the lun-

cheon. Katie and the other maids had decorated the
smaller dining room with fresh flowers and streamers.
Never had the cook's chicken salad been tastier, her
biscuits lighter, and the seven-layer cake frosted with
pink icing took the guests' breath away. Yet all through
the meal and the riverboat trip so hastily arranged,
Heather longed for everyone but Alice to be gone.
Finally the girls left, after praising Mrs. Templeton's
efforts until Heather felt ill.

In the safety of her room, they talked—Alice in her
blue gown curled up on a sofa, Heather in her rocker.
Only when she finished the whole miserable story did
Alice mysteriously say, "Can you hang on until next
spring?"

"I suppose I'll have to hang on until next summer
when I'm twenty-one," Heather despondently replied.
"Even then I may not be able to escape. Father will
never let me take a job and I won't marry any of the
men Adelaide parades before me."

"Cheer up," Alice told her. She reached into the reticule she'd dropped on a small table. "I have a letter
for you from Harry."

Heather's spine straightened as if she'd been struck
by lightning. "You *do*? Why didn't he write to me?"

"Read it and see. It's open because he told me to
read it first." The round blue eyes sparkled and Alice
beamed. "I'd like to hear it again. Read it out loud."

"All right." Heather unfolded the carefully written
pages and began.

"Dear Twin." She ignored the tightness of her throat
and continued.

"I'm not sending you the usual birthday present

'cause I'm saving for something a lot better, something you're going to like. That's the reason I'm sending this through Alice. Ever since you wrote and said you hadn't heard from me I've suspected Adelaide is intercepting my letters, although I naturally can't prove it. If she is, I don't want her to see this. She'd give it to Father and whew! Everything would go up in smoke.

"Anyway, I have a new friend. He's twenty-five, Irish and named Brian Boru O'Rourke, although the men in the logging camp call him Blarney and say he kissed the Blarney Stone. He found me hurt on the trail and packed me in and took care of me."

Heather looked at Alice. "He doesn't say how he got hurt." A worried frown wrinkled her forehead.

"I know, but he must be all right now. Go on." Alice gave a little bounce and two dimples showed in her round cheeks.

"Brian and I have acquired some land and a cabin in an interesting way that I'll tell you sometime. This means it won't take so long for me to save Alice's passage money." The letter fell to her lap and Heather exclaimed, "I'm so happy for you!" Yet a pang shot through her. She'd miss Alice so much.

"Don't stop reading," Alice prodded and continued to look secretive.

Heather picked up the letter again. "When I told Brian about Adelaide and how hard she's made it, driving me away and trying to turn Father against you, too, why he up and suggested a plan. He has some money, not a lot, but if we both work until snow flies then hole in at the cabin and start making furniture and adding a couple more rooms, he says by next spring we'll have money enough to bring Alice out here *and you, too*, Heather. That's why I'm saving every copper. You'll like Brian. He's the best thing. . ."

Heather cut off the eulogy by tossing the pages to the floor. She pulled Alice from the sofa and into a joyous dance. "We're going to Washington Territory. Can you believe it?"

Alice's flaxen hair tumbled from its moorings and hairpins flew. "I know. That's why I asked if you could hold out. Oh, Heather, could anything be more wonderful?"

"I've been asking God for help. Do you think He sent this Brian man to Harry?" Heather stopped in mid-stride.

"Why not?" Always practical, Alice smiled at her friend. "He's promised to take care of His children and that's us." She glanced out the window. "Oh, dear. Your father and Adelaide are back. Now don't give things away. Smooth down your dress and hair." She snatched up pins and anchored her own, then shooed Heather out the door.

They met Adelaide and Harrison on the stairs.

"Did you have a nice birthday?" Adelaide's brows rose in a knowing gesture.

"The best and happiest and most wonderful birthday a girl ever had," Heather bubbled. "Thank you for the party, Adelaide."

The woman bit her lip and stared but Harrison looked relieved, and when his daughter exuberantly flung her arms around him, he actually smiled with approval into her flushed face and returned the embrace.

three

Sustained by her secret, Heather Templeton began a time period in her life she privately told Alice could only be described as mealymouthed.

"Yes, Adelaide. No, Adelaide," she mimicked her own cowed voice then added in normal tones, "Not that it does much good. It's impossible to believe the difference between the way she orders me around and screams when Father's out of the house and the disgusting sweetness and hurt innocence she puts on for his benefit." She crossed her arms, left bare by the short, puffy sleeves of her white muslin gown, and stared out the window. Ripened fruit had long since replaced the blossoms that promised a bountiful harvest. Summer had melted into September, a long heat wave driven away by welcome rain. A few unusually cool nights had left leaves with a faint blush; before long the orange of autumn would paint the world in shades of yellows, golds and reds.

"You made it this far," Alice reminded her. In pink dimity, her round face above the round white collar reflected the tints and resembled a full-blown apple blossom. She giggled. "Good thing your stepmother doesn't know what we're planning. She'd feel it her Christian duty to spread the scandal all over New York State, especially to my parents."

A matching smile curved Heather's lips. "I'm glad

Harry wrote that absolutely meaningless letter to me here. I'm sure it had been opened before I got it."

Alice bounced on the sofa, her usual retreat. Her giggles turned to full-scale laughter but she sobered when Heather added, "Christian duty, nothing. You know she only attends church because Father's pew is one of the most prominent in the church and she can show off her fine clothing."

"Now, Sister Templeton, let us be charitable." Alice drew the corners of her mouth down and tried to look serious, a miserable attempt because of her naturally cheerful countenance. "We must look for the good in our fellowmen— fellowwomen? Come now, can't you think of anything good about Adelaide?" She sighed audibly and continued her impromptu sermon. "We must look past the obvious and discover what lies deep within the soul of man—"

A well-aimed pillow cut her short. Yet although it had been in fun, Heather thought a lot about what her friend had said. Surely Adelaide couldn't be bad all the way through. "God, I'm going to try to discover something, even if it's only one thing, about her that's admirable and true." The vow resulted in a close scrutiny that ended with Adelaide snapping, "Why do you stare at me, missy? What am I, the pig-faced lady?"

Heather gave up and retreated to the sanctuary of her room to reread Harry's last letter, one that had *not* come to the Templeton address. Heather thought of her frantic appeal earlier in the summer, her plea for Harry to write a noncommittal letter. When he had started sending messages via Alice and no letter came to the house, it brought forth a tirade from Adelaide on how she'd known all along he didn't care a thing even for his sister and the lack of letters proved it. She ended by vindictively saying, "Harrison, this just goes to show how right you were in laying down an edict that Harry would either serve his country honorably or no longer be your son. Not that he won't come crawling home sometime." Heather had seen the pain in her father's eyes but he only scowled and nodded, then remarked they wouldn't discuss Harry. It had taken every ounce of willpower not to produce the steady string of encouraging letters that told how much her brother cared for her, how hard he was working to free her from bondage.

Insight into what made Adelaide unendurable came in an odd way and through Alice. She hurried in one crisp October afternoon, politely greeted the mistress of the house and escaped to Heather's room. Even before she dropped her warm pelisse and removed her bonnet, she said in a low voice that couldn't penetrate the heavy bedroom door, "Just wait 'til you hear." Long experience had shown the girls that they never knew when Adelaide would barge in unannounced.

Heather started from her rocker but her friend imperiously waved her toward the sofa next to her. "I don't want her to hear." She slipped out of her outdoor clothing and let the pelisse fall carelessly to the floor, tossing her bonnet on a nearby table. "I found out about Adelaide."

"You *what*?"

The excited Alice leaned close and kept her voice to a whisper. "You'll never guess why she's so greedy and determined to get the money that you and Harry should inherit if anything happens to your father." A solemn look crossed her face and her blue eyes shadowed. "An old friend of Mother's came to visit and I overheard them talking."

"Alice, you weren't eavesdropping, were you?" The idea horrified Heather.

"Not guilty." Her flaxen curls shook impatiently. "Mother asked me to bring in tea. Besides, the woman didn't seem to care who heard."

"What did she say?"

"It's kind of sad. Adelaide's parents were so poor that half the time the children didn't have enough to eat. One winter they nearly froze to death in an unheated house. She had to wear ragged clothing and all the other children jeered at her. According to our visitor, Adelaide said someday she'd be in a position so she'd never be cold or hungry and no one on earth would dare laugh."

"It's hard to picture Adelaide with that background, seeing her now," Heather mused while her heart went out to the poverty-stricken, tormented child.

"I know. She's always so perfectly turned out. I guess that's why." Alice made a face. "It still doesn't make me like her any better but I can see why she's like she is. Remember what the preacher said last Sunday about fear? That it drives people to do all kinds of unbelievable things?" She shivered and clasped her arms across her chest.

"Are you cold? Wait." Heather sprang up, snatched a warm quilt from a cupboard and handed it to Alice. "Shall I light the lamps?"

"No. It's cozy this way." Alice snuggled into the

folds of the quilt. "Heather, I know what the preacher meant."

"You?" This couldn't be Alice, the bold, Alice, the laughing, confessing such a thing. "What are you afraid of?"

"That something will happen to Harry and I'll never get to see him again." Her voice sounded muffled.

"Alice Freeman, that's wicked. You know God's watching over us all! Why, didn't He send Mr. O'Rourke to help Harry be able to raise our passage money? You know God loves us and wants us to have the best in our lives."

"I know."

"Then why are you afraid?" Heather held her breath, sensing great importance lay in the answer to her question.

"Because God doesn't always give us what we think is the best."

Heather tried to still her tumbling thoughts. "When He doesn't, it's just that He has something even better for us," she faltered. "Alice, surely you don't want to go to Washington Territory and marry my brother if it isn't God's will!"

Alice didn't reply for a long time. When she did, Heather could scarcely believe she heard right.

"I'm afraid I do." A plump, white hand crept out from beneath the quilt and clutched Heather's arm. "I can't explain what even the thought of losing Harry means to me." She choked and swiped at her eyes with her free hand. "Someday, when you love someone more than life itself, you'll know how I feel."

Heather sat speechless. She'd always known of the

fondness between her twin and Alice but never had she suspected the depths of love in her merry companion's heart.

Alice tightened her grip. "It has to be that way. Unless a woman's heart is filled with that kind of feeling, how could she leave her family and cleave unto her husband, as the Bible says?" She blinked and a tremulous smile chased away sadness. "Maybe you'd better light the lamps now. I'm sure God will take care of Harry and us, and we'll be together in the spring. It's just that the years have been so long since he left. It seems like spring will never come, but it always does, doesn't it?"

Shaken by her friend's disclosures, Heather nodded. "Yes, and it can't come any too soon for me."

A new maturity rested on her friend when she slipped from beneath her quilt and stood. With her usual practical manner she smoothed down her gown, donned her pelisse and bonnet, and grinned the infectious grin that never failed to make Heather smile. "Remember, when Adelaide is obnoxious—and she will be, worse luck—try to picture a miserable child who slaved to better herself so she could escape unpleasantness, just as you're going to flee unhappiness next spring."

Alice's advice proved invaluable. Heather did her best to do just what her friend recommended. Adelaide's bursts of temperament continued but her stepdaughter's attitude changed. By Christmas, the new sweetness that surrounded Heather gradually brought about an uneasy truce.

A package arrived from Harry: beaded moccasins with a note they were handmade by the Indians who lived not far from his cabin. Adelaide sniffed and called them heathenish but took care not to say anything in front of her husband. A slight thaw toward his absent son had come when Heather happily reported he had a steady job, was building on to his little house, and planning to cultivate his land for a garden in the spring.

Heather saw fear in her stepmother's eyes. Would it do any good to assure her neither of the twins wanted to deprive her of a share of the Templeton money? Heather sadly shook her head. Adelaide would never believe it, conditioned as she was by her own background with its survival of the strong clawing to get what one wanted.

The cold winter days gave Heather time to consider many things. Now her window overlooked deep snow, shutting out the future, closing in the present, making it a time to reflect. She faced the unwelcome thought of what would happen should Harry and his friend fail to earn passage money for both girls. Alice must be the one to go if it came to that. But what could she do, Heather wondered. Wrapped in a warm robe, feet in her cherished moccasins, she considered. "I won't marry to get away from home," she determined. "I can run a house but until I'm twenty-one, Father won't let me take a job. Even afterwards, it will mean a complete break if I refuse to obey his commands." She sighed. "Domestic work, sewing, laundry." She ticked off the available occupations for women on her fingers. "Teaching? Perhaps. Maybe I could get work as a nurse. It's starting to become respectable because of the women who served in the hospitals and camps during the War, but Father would never consent."

She shook herself. The brightest future actually lay in Washington Territory. With so few women compared with the number of men, she'd have a choice of either teaching or nursing. "I won't let Harry and Alice support me," she proudly vowed. A mischievous smile lighted her sober face. "According to Harry, if I choose to marry there will be a line of suitors beating a path to the cabin. Dear me, even thirteen and fourteen-year-old girls are betrothed, Harry says, usually to men twice and three times their age." She stared at her beautifully-made moccasins and her smile faded, remembering Harry's honest confession that some of the men took Indian mates, with or without the benefit of clergy.

"I don't know what I'll find there, God," she prayed. "I just hope those of us who love You can be candles in the wilderness. Harry says good women are sorely needed, as much for their influence as the fact men need wives. Please, help Alice and me to shine for You."

Heather closed her eyes but couldn't conjure up an accurate picture of her brother's home in spite of his letters. She knew tall trees surrounded it but no clear image came to mind. She'd just have to wait and see it for herself. She had less trouble imagining Brian Boru O'Rourke, the kindhearted Irishman with the nickname Blarney. She'd seen a few young Irish lads on the street who faintly resembled Harry's description of his friend. A composite of them gave her a fair idea of curly red hair, laughing blue eyes, a wide grin. A faint stirring within made her blush. Would he like her, this son of the Emerald Isle?

"Why not?" She stretched. "He obviously likes

Harry and I'm part of him."

❧

Winter persisted and grated on nerves. Adelaide re-
sumed her well-bred torture, blond head high and eyes
guileless when she complained to her husband of his
daughter's actions. Heather knew part of it came from
the forced inactivity. Her stepmother always grew more
unbearable when confined to the house because of in-
clement weather. The rest she attributed to her father's
interest in Harry's doings. That flash of fear in
Adelaide's eyes at Christmas grew stronger and it took
all Heather's skill to evade the vengeful woman.

Even Alice's visits were not a complete success.
Some of her fears attacked Heather. They discussed
freely what they'd do in the event their passage money
wasn't forthcoming. Once Alice wrinkled her nose
and said, "If the absolute worst happens, I'm not going to lose my chance of going to Harry."

"How could you help it?"

"I'll sign up to go with Asa Mercer." Her full lips
set in a straight line.

"Asa Mercer!" Heather raised her eyebrows in disapproval. "You mean that man who took some young
women to Puget Sound in 1864? Alice Freeman, have
you lost your senses?"

Every flaxen curl bobbed when she shook her head.
"No, I've just come to them! Mercer's president of
the Territorial University at Seattle. I've been reading
everything I can find about him. He recognized the
need for teachers and wives in the Territory and that
there are thousands more unmarried girls and women
here in the East than men because of the War. Many of

them, especially in New England, don't have any way to make a living. Neither do the war widows who have orphaned children." Her face warmed with enthusiasm. "Heather, those eleven young woman, most from Lowell in Massachusetts, became teachers. Some married and the rest undoubtedly will. Don't you see? If I have to go that way, I will. He's getting ready to take a far larger number. He left Seattle March last year and intends to take hundreds of girls and women on his next trip! They'll become teachers and seamstresses and housemaids but eventually marry." She clasped her hands and her eyes sparkled. "Think about going with me, will you?"

"Me?" Heather gasped and her skin tingled at the prospect. "Father would never forgive me."

"He won't forgive you no matter how you go," Alice told her. "At least think about it." She hugged her friend and left before Heather could gather her wits enough for a scathing reply.

Suddenly Heather became an avid reader of the newspapers. She found plenty about Asa Mercer and his proposed boatload of brides, as some called the expedition. Some saw it as an affront to everything decent and moral. Others sympathetically predicted the gentle pioneers would bring culture to the West. Doubt about the character of any widow or maiden who embarked on such a voyage hung in the air. From coast to coast the newspapers milked the story for every last drop of notoriety. Because of aspersions cast on the motives of both Mercer and possible participants, many young women summarily cancelled their passage.

Now Alice and Heather spent most of their time together discussing bits and pieces of news. The *S. S. Continental*, a screw steamer built in Philadelphia in 1862, had been secured and offered good lighting, ventilation, pleasant staterooms and a variety of other amenities, including medical service, a library, and sewing machines, plus lifeboats and preservers sufficient for all passengers. Little by little, Heather unwillingly grew intrigued with the whole idea, until at last she consented to go if necessary.

Alice immediately said, "Good. Now let me tell you what I've been thinking. Who knows if Mr. Mercer will be able to make more trips in the future? Why don't we go now? The *Continental* is scheduled to sail on January 16th."

"But that's not even two weeks away!" Heather protested.

"I know." Alice dimpled.

"Why, Harry and Mr. O'Rourke have probably already secured our passage money," Heather burst out. "Why should we go before they send it to us?"

"If we can get there on our own, think of how much better off we'll all be," Alice argued, cheeks pink and eyes flaming with zeal. "If you won't go with me, I'll go alone." She slowly pulled papers from her reticule. "I might as well confess. I signed us up. We'll sell our jewelry."

"Well, of all the. . . ." Speech failed Heather.

Alice only smirked. "I told the interviewers my sister, oh, I added "to be" under my breath, wasn't able to come but showed them a picture and said you were of good moral character."

Heather didn't know whether to laugh or shake her.

"What will Harry say?"

A faint shadow crept across Alice's face. "I don't think he will like it much. Once I mentioned Asa Mercer in a letter to see how he felt about him. He wrote back the man's name was held for good and evil. He didn't say not to come that way," she blandly continued.

"Why should he? Who but you would come up with such a ludicrous plan?"

With the quick change of mood that made her so appealing, the flaxen-haired girl let her shoulders slump. "I've just got to go now," she said. Her voice quivered. "I don't even know why. It's like something is compelling me."

"Are you sure we aren't running before God?"

Alice's eyes gleamed at the word *we*. She threw her arms around her friend. "You won't regret it. I promise."

"I already do," Heather said sourly. Not until Alice had gone, the gaudy locket and other trinkets hidden in her reticule, did she remember she hadn't answered Heather.

Torn between guilt and relief, Heather seesawed between rushing to Alice's and reneging on her feeble-minded agreement and the siren song of freedom that sang in her ears. The song won, released to full volume after an acrimonious encounter with Adelaide worse than anything that had gone before. A tearful recital at the dinner table ended with Harrison Templeton turning glacial. His edict fell like cubes of ice, bruising his unjustly accused daughter's heart.

"I have had all I will stand," he told her. "For a time

you appeared to be more tractable, willing to overcome the terrible temper that causes you to wound Adelaide." His brows met in a fierce line. Not a trace of understanding or love showed beneath them. "For some time I have considered a course of action so abhorrent I felt I couldn't bring myself to take it. Now your rebellion makes clear what I must do. You can only blame yourself. One month from today, unless Adelaide tells me there is a decided improvement and that you are subordinate to her and carry out her orders, I will arrange for you to be taken from the city in a closed carriage. We will tell the servants and our friends only that you are away for a time."

Heather's heart leaped. Being sent to some relative, no matter how distant or unpleasant, couldn't be worse than her present situation. Icy horror descended on her when her father went on in a voice so devoid of emotion it sounded dead.

"Several miles from here there is an institution for wayward young women, those who refuse to honor and obey their parents. You will be taken there and remain until you repent of your sins, learn to appreciate how much you have given up and become the Christian young woman your mother taught you to be. In the meantime, I will arrange a suitable marriage."

She opened her mouth to protest.

"Silence!" Fury returned to his voice and his face grew mottled. "Now get out of my sight."

She stood and clutched at her chair for support. Some of the courage she had inherited from the man who condemned her without a hearing shattered the spell induced by his decree. Scorn laced her words. "One

day you will know the truth and it will be too late."
She felt strength, born of innocence and fed by
righteousness, sweep through her. She pointed at
Adelaide who sat quietly, unable to hide her victory.

"The serpent you brought into this house has driven
away your son and turned you against your daughter.
When the time is right, she will turn on you—and no
one will be here to help you, Father. Then you will cry
out the truth but no one will hear."

Heather knew the shock of her daring to stand against
him that kept her father silent would break into uncon-
trollable rage. She gathered her skirts and ran, thanking God with all her might for Alice's interfering bold-
ness in providing a way out when the gates of her
father's home and heart had clanged shut behind her.

four

Harry Templeton's joy knew no bounds when he received the letter from Alice and Heather saying they could hardly bear to wait until spring. "Work hard, dearest," Alice had written. "I pray for you daily and will be the best wife any man ever had. How can I help it with a husband like you?"

Heather's shorter message simply read, "You'll never know what this means to me."

"But I do," Harry quietly told Brian. "For the first time in all the months since I left home, I feel happy and safe about her. I didn't trust Adelaide from the moment she snared my father. Besides, twins sense each other's feelings more than most."

"I believe it. You've been for telling me about it plenty of times," Brian retorted, but his broad grin and fun-filled gaze showed genuine affection for the younger man. In the weeks since they'd moved into the partially-completed cabin, worked, hunted and fished together, bonds akin to what Brian knew he'd have felt for a brother had developed. He'd learned to listen for the cheery whistle that announced Harry's arrival, to appreciate the returning strength and dogged determination that won the respect of the loggers. It had taken the combined efforts of the crew to hold young Templeton back from trying every hard and dangerous job. They succeeded only until the doctor reluctantly admitted Harry appeared to have recuperated. Both he and Brian welcomed overtime and stashed away every extra copper that didn't go for basic food and clothing. Now and then they reluctantly dipped into their growing hoard to purchase necessities for the cabin. To their delight, the entire logging crew, headed up by Miller, appeared at their cleared area one summer day when extreme fire danger from an unseasonable spell of heat forced them from the woods.

"Thought we'd give a hand," the burly logger said. By the end of the day, another large room had been added in a twinkling. The men refused to take pay. "Just introduce us to that sister of yours when she comes." His eyes twinkled. "'course, I s'pose Blarney will steal her before the rest of us have a chance, bein' right here on the scene and all."

Brian's irrepressible grin broke out and his teeth shone white against deeply tanned skin. They made his eyes bluer and his short curls redder than ever. "Faith, and how'd I be for standing a chance against that handsome mug of yours, Miller?" The entire crew howled. Big Miller might be; handsome he was not.

The logger laughed with the rest. Brian had found so long as the men left booze alone, few fights occurred in the bunkhouse or woods. Only when they went to town and got "likkered up," as the straw boss grumpily called it, did meanness and argumentativeness crop up. Then they fought with or without cause, unceasingly and joyously. Brian and Harry had long since refused to go with them, glad for their work on Harry's place to use as an excuse.

"I wasn't raised to drink," Harry said quietly the first

time the crew invited him. After the usual unmerciful joshing the men turned to Brian.

"How about you, Blarney?"

"I'm full enough of malarkey without tipping the bottle, I'm for thinking," he told them, knowing he and his new friend got away with it because they had already proved in the woods they were neither cowards nor sissies.

Miller eyed the pair with disfavor. "You ain't gonna start preachin' to us on the evils of drink, are you?"

"We'll leave the preaching to Clifton," Brian told him. "Say boys, he's trying hard to get a church going closer to us than Seattle. How about helping?"

"You mean a church-raisin'?" Miller scratched his head. "I've heard of barn-raisin's and house-raisin's, but never no church-raisin'." His face split in a grin. "Might not be so bad at that. Bet the homesteaders around would all come. We'd get some good female cooking."

"Something wrong with camp fare?" the cook hollered. A glint in his eyes foretold an unhappy fate for anyone who complained.

"Naw, you're the best flapjack flipper and steak fryer in the Territory," Miller said. "Womenfolk fix fancy stuff, though." He loftily added, obviously for the cook's benefit, "Nice for a change but a real he-man sure wouldn't want that kinda food very often."

The result of Brian's suggestion was a workday that ended with a plain log building in a clearing not far from Harry's place. Reverend Clifton, pale in spite of exposure to the northwest sun, announced services the next Sunday. To Brian's amazement, enough people came to fill every wooden bench. Overjoyed, too, was the young minister who had come from New England in hopes of having his own church and congregation but with few finances and less idea of how to go about it.

"You'll never know what this means to me," he fervently told his diverse congregation. Loggers with slicked back hair and spanking-clean clothes elbowed homesteaders. A few pioneer wives and a handful of wide-eyed children whose faces showed evidence of a recent hard scrubbing stood out like occasional blossoms in a field of weeds. Just after the first song burst forth, a shadow darkened the open doorway.

"Well, would ja look at that!" Miller, who although uncomfortable had good-naturedly led the band of loggers who agreed to come, poked Brian in the ribs with a muscular elbow.

Brian turned and glanced back. A tall Indian clad in buckskins stood just behind one of the most beautiful girls the Irishman had ever seen. Dusky hair parted in the middle formed two long braids that hung over her shoulders and framed the pure oval of her face. Shining dark eyes beneath silky brows surveyed the assembly. Brian had seen the half-curious, half-frightened expression in the eyes of the deer who came to inspect his cabin. For a moment he met her gaze, but it swept on and rested on Reverend Clifton, the first to regain his wits.

"Welcome." He raised his hand in greeting. "Men, would you push over and give our visitors a place to sit?"

When the congregation didn't move but continued

to gape, a frown crossed Clifton's face but with a fluid movement, Harry Templeton stood, yanked Brian to his feet and to one side. Without speaking, he motioned to the two striking figures, then hissed, "Move over, Miller."

The logger did so, so vigorously he nearly shoved his neighbor off the end of the bench. The two Indians glided to the vacant spots and seated themselves, backs ramrod-straight. The tall man sat with arms crossed, listening without speaking. The girl next to him kept her gaze on the slim-fingered hands clasped in the lap of her fringed buckskin skirt. From the place hastily made by those across and back one pew, Brian and Harry had an excellent view. In Brian's travels he had seen all types of people: South Sea islanders in colorful garments; black and brown and white and yellow inhabitants of the world. Few had impressed him the way these two did. Never had he encountered such natural dignity.

If their presence disturbed Clifton, it didn't show. After a few more songs, he opened his Bible and began to expound. A vague disappointment filled Brian. He could count the times on one hand and have fingers left over that he'd heard preaching in the past years, yet something didn't feel right. He tried to identify it and finally decided Reverend Clifton needed to trade in his Eastern style of preaching for a simple telling of the Gospel learned at mothers' knees. The lecture being given was more suited to a ministerial convention than a gathering of loggers, homesteaders, and the two Indians.

How much did they understand? Brian looked around

the room and his spirits fell. Harry looked equally disappointed. Miller and the loggers' bold stares never left the preacher but a cocked eyebrow here and there and some downturned mouths confirmed Brian's evaluation. Mothers quieted their children when the discourse went on and on.

At the height of the sermon, the tall Indian rose, arms still crossed over his chest. Clifton hesitated but when the visitor made no move to leave, he faltered and stopped. "Is—is there something wrong?" His pale face flushed and sweat broke out on his forehead.

"You are minister." A little gasp ran through the congregation. Until now, it had been impossible to know if either of the Indians understood or spoke English.

"Why, yes." Clifton drew himself up.

"You know Jesus, Son of Great Spirit?"

Brian leaned forward in the deathly stillness, wondering if he were dreaming. It felt unreal, this cross-examination of a man in clerical black by the one in buckskin.

"Of course I know Jesus." Some of Clifton's aplomb returned.

"You no speak of Him." He turned to the girl, whose face reflected his features. "Come." Quiet fell, so deafening the light footsteps of soft moccasins sounded loud in the little church as the tall Indian and the girl who must be his daughter walked out, dignity intact.

Brian would have laughed at anyone who told him he'd ever witness such a happening. Everyone present must know Reverend Clifton had been bested by a man considered a savage. How had he come to know the white man's God? Was he a believer? Would he or the girl return? Probably not. The Indians had evidently come seeking to know more of God's Son and had been treated to a well-presented but personal view of the speaker.

A verse Brian had found marked in Captain Haines' old Bible came to mind. *"If a son shall ask bread of any of you that is a father, will he give him a stone?"** The Indian who could well be a chief, if his carriage and demeanor spoke truly, had left the church without the Bread of Life and was wise enough to know it. What of the others who needed Jesus so much in their lives? Miller. The loggers. The homesteaders. Himself. In the moments between the departure of the dark-skinned couple and Clifton's recovery, a pang went through Brian. It had taken the quiet challenge of a man considered pagan to awaken the need in his own heart for the God of his parents.

He snapped back to attention when Reverend Clifton hastily announced, "We will close with singing Come Thou Fount of Every Blessing. I will line it out and you may follow." He had a pleasant voice, good for song-leading. When the song ended he lifted his hands and pronounced a benediction, mainly concerned with the gladness that should be in every heart for a beautiful day. Brian found himself waiting for a sentence asking forgiveness or recognizing the validity of the Indian's statements, perhaps a petition asking for another chance. It didn't come. Reverend Clifton rolled out an "Amen," and the service ended. The worshippers spilled out into the clearing. Brian found himself next to Miller again.

* Luke 11:11

"Whadda ya think?" the logger demanded, fist planted on his muscled thighs.

Unwilling to condemn the young minister at first hearing, Brian responded, "He's for being a good speaker."

Miller snorted. "Yeah, but he doesn't say nothin'." He grimaced. "I ain't much for redskins and never thought I'd sit next to one in church, even if she is pretty as a spotted pony, but I couldn't help admirin' him. I ain't much for church, either. Reckon you guessed that. Anyway, that young preacher needs to listen to what the chief said or me and the boys won't be back. We got better things to do than listen to a high-falutin' talk we can't understand and don't want to." He dropped his ham-fist on Brian's shoulder with a blow that would stagger a lesser man, grinned and marched off.

In different words, Harry pretty much repeated Miller's sentiments later that afternoon. From the time they made the cabin habitable and moved in, they conscientiously observed the Sabbath by doing only the necessary food preparation, and lounging the rest of the day. "Mother always said God meant for us to just enjoy the day and Him," the younger man said. "Makes sense, too. If a man keeps going seven days a week, he's no better than a beast of the field or forest."

Sometimes they hiked; they often found a stream and came home with a mess of shining fish. Their bonds of friendship strengthened in those Sunday afternoons. Both men enjoyed reading and Harry usually wrote to Alice and Heather, especially if the weather turned rainy. This afternoon the men grabbed cold meat and biscuits, washed them down with clear, cold water, and by mutual agreement, headed into the woods. Another trait in common was their love of the forest.

"We'll do some more clearing when we can," Harry mused a little later when they reached a shining stream and worked their way down. Each week they explored a little farther from home and today they followed the stream until it took a deep bend, then curiously rounded it. "Look, Brian." Harry excitedly pointed. They stood on a little knoll. Beneath them the stream joined a larger one in a rush of white water. Close to the point they joined, a small encampment of Indian teepees picturesquely filled the landscape.

"I'll bet our visitors came from here." Brian peered to see if he could recognize the tall Indian and the girl among the figures below. "They must be friendly or they wouldn't have come to the church. I thought the Indians were on reservations."

"The coastal Indians signed treaties in '55," Harry told him. "The Yakima chief Kamiakin led in war until '58 when the Indians lost a battle near Four Lakes in the eastern part of the Territory. I don't know what these are doing here. Shall we go find out?" He quickly added, "Might as well. We've been spotted."

The small village of Indians proved to be neither welcoming nor hostile. Impassive brown faces turned toward the two men and away, except for the children who stared and a few dogs that growled just enough to establish boundaries. Things changed when they reached the center of the settlement and the Indian who had walked out of church stepped from the largest teepee. He didn't speak but folded his arms as he had done that morning and waited.

"We stumbled on your camp while fishing," Brian quickly explained. He held up their catch, silvery fish strung on a forked branch.

"You are welcome. I am Chief Running Wolf. These are my people."

"I am Brian O'Rourke and this is my friend, Harry Templeton." On impulse he added, "I am glad you and your daughter came to church." He looked straight into the chief's eyes. "I am also glad you said what you did."

"Minister make much talk, say nothing," he echoed Miller's evaluation of the long sermon.

Brian couldn't help laughing and saw a fleeting look of amusement creep into the midnight-black eyes. "Reverend Clifton is young and has much to learn," he told the chief.

Harry spoke for the first time, hazel eyes eager and a big smile on his face. "How did you hear about Jesus, Son of God—of the Great Spirit?"

"Daughter Crying Dove hear white man talk while Chief Running Wolf hunting. He come to village, say white man and red man are brothers." An inscrutable expression swept over the bronzed face. "She believe what she hear."

"And you, Chief?" Brian softly asked. It suddenly felt important to know what went on behind the well-adjusted mask Chief Running Wolf wore to hide his feelings.

For a long time the statuesque Indian faced his visitors. Then he turned, looked into the forest, above them the shining cap of Mount Rainier. "My people call it *mountain that was God*. It looks at red man and white but no calls them brothers."

The patter of flying feet heralded the arrival of the girl in buckskins. "Father?"

"Daughter, Crying Dove. Chief Running Wolf no have son." A flash of longheld pain broke the impassive face for such a short moment Brian wondered if he had really seen it.

Brian bowed in the girl's direction. "You are a Christian?"

She nodded, after an anxious look at her father.

"We are glad." Brian sensed the visit had gone on long enough and quickly held his hand out to the chief. Running Wolf briefly took it, then Harry's. Crying Dove only smiled, but when the men reached the little knoll and turned, she still stood next to her father, her face turned toward the white visitors.

"She's a beauty. You can see why some of the white men marry Indian girls," Harry observed and swung around the bend, leaving the village behind. His face darkened. "There are also too many men who just take them without marriage."

"What happens when they tire of them?"

"I understand the girls are outcasts. They won't be accepted by the whites and the Indians don't want them back. It's the same for the children born of such unions, even when the man marries the girl according to white custom." He sighed. "Poor little tykes. Sometimes it's hard to see why God allows men's wickedness to ruin the lives of innocent children."

For a moment Brian saw himself at not quite eight, far from home, always hungry, lonely, miserable.

Memories clutched at his strong throat. "Neither do I."

Before the next Sunday, Reverend Clifton rode out to the logging camp on a sad-eyed, sorry-looking horse someone had cheated him into buying. "I'll be holding services next Sunday," he announced to the men who had just come in from the woods. "I hope to see you all there."

Brian knew by the furtive looks the crew exchanged that hope was doomed to failure. He and Harry started for their own place and Clifton rode down the now-defined trail behind them.

"You'll come, won't you?" he pleaded, eyes strangely colorless in his pale face. His mousy hair lay hidden beneath the broad-brimmed black hat.

Brian sighed, but nodded.

An impish look came to Harry's grimy, sweat-stained face. "Reverend, are you calling on all those who attended last week?"

"Why, yes." He rubbed his chin with one finger. "The Lord has told us to preach the Gospel to all."

"Then you'll be needing directions to the Indian camp."

Brian almost burst at the cat-in-the-cream look on Harry's usually innocent countenance. He bit his lip hard when he glanced at Reverend Clifton. The minister looked the way a bully of a sailor looked the day Brian had been forced to teach him a lesson and did it in one hard blow to the solar plexus. The Irishman knew how it felt. A mean horse had once kicked him in the stomach and left him feeling caved in.

Now Clifton stammered, "Why, after last Sunday do

you really think that's wise?"

Harry's eyes grew round with pretended shock. "My goodness, it's not what I think. You're the minister and you said the Gospel must go to all." He ducked his head and when he looked up again he continued. "The girl, Crying Dove, is a Christian."

"She is!" Again the minister appeared jolted. All trace of his reluctance fled. "In that case, she is one of my parishioners, isn't she?" He flung his hand toward the vast wilderness surrounding them. "I wonder what my friends back East will say when they learn how many miles my parish encompasses."

The sheer effrontery of the man sidetracked any answer and silence reigned supreme until the trio reached Harry's cabin. "If you'd like to wait, we'll clean up and you can eat supper with us," Brian offered. Even to himself he couldn't name the odd reluctance with which he gave the invitation or the unaccountable relief that came when Clifton hesitated, eyed the snug cabin in the clearing, then said,

"Perhaps I should visit the Indian village, as you suggested. Can I make it before dark?"

"Easily, if your horse doesn't lie down and die on the way," Harry solemnly told him. He indicated the trail. "Just keep going and going. You'll see where we followed it last Sunday afternoon."

Sharp suspicion leaped to Clifton's eyes. "What were *you* doing there?" Again Brian felt the same funny niggling inside.

"Stumbled on it while fishing."

"Oh." Evidently satisfied, the minister turned his horse in the direction Harry pointed. Just before he reached the limits of cleared land he turned and waved. His pale face gleamed in the late afternoon sunlight. He vanished into the woods, sagging horse and all.

"Somehow, I'm for wishing you hadn't told him about the village," Brian impulsively burst out, gaze still on the opening into the forest.

"Whyever not?" Harry looked astonished. "You don't think the Indians will hurt him, do you? Chief Running Wolf might not think much of his brand of preaching but he's not on the warpath."

Brian's blue eyes darkened with thought, like Puget Sound when the orange sun dropped behind the horizon and left it lapping velvet waves on the shore. "No." He couldn't explain his uneasiness, yet long after Harry shrugged and went to clean up, the former sailor stood looking in the direction Clifton had gone.

five

"Blarney, I'm worried." Harry Templeton laid down the pages of a letter and scowled.

"Alice hasn't changed her mind, has she?"

"No, but blamed if she isn't asking all kinds of questions about Asa Mercer and his doings." The scowl deepened. "You don't suppose she's got some fool notion in her head about contacting him do you? It would be just like her!"

"How can she?" Brian asked reasonably. He finished greasing his cork boots with deer tallow to keep them supple and waterproofed as much as possible. With the passing of summer, a gray mist of rain and fog had swept in alongside September. "Aren't the girls and women who sign on with Mercer required to be eligible for marriage?" He chuckled deep in his throat. "Seems I've been for hearing Miller and some of the others bragging that they're going to snag some of the Mercer girls."

Harry shook his tousled head emphatically. "The passengers don't have to sign anything. Those that do choose to marry right away are allowed to do so and the way I hear it, the grooms are responsible for the passage money. The others are guaranteed jobs teaching, housecleaning or sewing." Pride warred with alarm in his young face. "If Alice figured she could get away with it, she'd stow away and save the money it will cost for her fare."

"Surely your sister wouldn't agree to such a wild scheme. From what you've said of her, she's pretty steady, isn't she?"

"She always was, but now—" Harry tapped the letter. "I can see Adelaide's up to her old tricks. Alice is furious but what can she do? Blarney, do you think I ought to go see how things are?"

"No. You won't be twenty-one until next summer. Neither will your sister. Legally, she belongs to your father until then. If you showed up, it might even make things worse." To turn his friend's dark thoughts he asked, "What do you actually know about Mercer and his schemes, anyway?"

"Angel and devil," came the instantaneous response. Harry let out a great sigh and leaned back in a comfortable chair, one of their more recent purchases. Brian watched his partner's gaze travel around the cabin. The logs had been securely chinked with moss and mud in the summer that dried to mortar. Sweet-smelling and left to weather outside, whitewash on the inside lightened and brightened the room. So did the cheery fire in the rough-stone fireplace built from great chunks of rock painstakingly unearthed and hauled to the cabin on an old sledge. After the first few times the men pulled it, they mutually agreed to invest in a team of horses strong enough to pull heavy loads and broken to the saddle. In the generous spirit of pioneering, the logging crew and homesteaders' wives, though few in number, had banded together and produced bright cotton curtains for the windows on each side of the heavy plank door and in the two rooms designated for sleeping. The cabin in the clearing bore mute witness to the generosity of the rough people. A huge bearskin rug lay on the floor in front of the fireplace, contributed by one of the men who brought down a giant of an animal, skillfully removed the pelt and cured it. The wooden beds Brian and Harry had constructed and filled with layer on layer of cedar boughs, hid under gorgeous patchwork quilts the kindly wives had secretly made at the same time they gathered to quilt for Reverend Clifton.

Strange that Harry's description of Asa Mercer brought the minister to mind. Brian had no time to pursue the thought.

"Depending on who you ask, Mercer is a man of great wisdom, determined to help enrich and ensure the future of Seattle and the surrounding area—or immoral and worthy of hanging." Harry stretched and firelight glinted in his hazel eyes. "Territorial Governor Pickering and the Massachusetts Governor John Andrew both endorse Mercer. So do others. Yet I just don't know. I'm not sure I want my fiancee or sister involved in any way."

"You may be for blowing up a storm on the horizon that will never rage," Brian reminded him. "Same as happens at sea. Sometimes gales come out of harmless-looking clouds but often as not, they sail on by."

"You don't know Alice," Harry darkly reminded, but a cheerful grin replaced his frown. "That's one of the reasons I love her. If there's an unpredictable thing to be done, she does it."

"Life will never be dull with such a colleen," Brian agreed. "Your sister keeps a more even keel?"

"She's never had a chance to do anything else, but I'll not predict what might happen when she gets out here." He sighed again and a wistful note colored his voice. "I just wish it were six months from now. We'd have the passage money and the girls would be on their way."

"Winter will be for passing soon," Brian comforted, yet the same minor note in Harry's words touched him. He wanted Alice and Heather to come, yet it meant the end of a way of life he'd never before known and hated to see stop. Ever since he and Harry moved into the cabin, they'd worked like well-matched horses pulling together without a hitch. Brian disliked the idea of returning to the bunkhouse when Heather Templeton came and needed the room he now occupied. He abruptly stood. "Harry, if there's a bit of money left in the pouch after we pay the girls' passage, I'd like to buy a corner of your land. Enough to build a shanty and still be close without interfering."

"Absolutely not." Harry leaped to his feet, mouth set in a hard line.

Brian's mouth dropped open. He hadn't meant to offend the lad. Bitterness filled him. Harry obviously meant to cling to what was his and let his mate go empty-handed. "Then we'll speak of it no more."

"We *will* speak of it." Never had Brian seen the younger man angrier. "You think I'd sell you land? I thought you knew me better than that."

The Irishman felt like he'd been slammed into a battering ram by the hands of a hundred strong men. He half-turned toward the door, seeking to escape. Harry's voice stopped him.

"If it weren't for you, I'd have no place, no way to bring Alice and Heather." The words came muffled by emotion. "The deed may say Harry Templeton but this cabin and clearing belong as much to Blarney O'Rourke and always will. I thought you knew that. If it makes you feel better, I'll have your name put on the deed to the property."

The deep hurt in the offer made Brian whirl, blue eyes soft with repentance. He started to explain. Paused. Harry must never know the betrayal his friend had felt. The open face showed beyond doubt the chasm such an admission would create.

"It's a dunderhead I'm for being," Brian confessed. His hand shot out. "Come help me pick a spot for my castle, will you?"

Relief and a gleaming smile restored Harry to normalcy. He gripped Brian's hand and followed him outside. They paced every inch of the "Templeton-O'Rourke Estates," as Harry laughingly dubbed them, and settled on the northwest corner, now choked with gigantic trees, salal, Oregon grape, and ferns.

"I'll build facing east," Brian decided. "The rising sun and snowcapped Mount Rainier will greet me each morning."

"Better plan to have an extra room in your castle," Harry slyly advised. "When you get a wife, she will be for wanting a sleeping room separate from the living and cooking room." His imitation of Brian's Irish manner of speaking made them both laugh before Harry added, "We can sell off some of our trees for lumber once we use what's needed for building but unless times get mighty hard, I'd like to keep some forested areas for the deer and other animals."

"Agreed, but we'll have to fence off our garden if we want anything from it."

In the planning, Harry's concern for Alice getting involved in an escapade dwindled—until her next letter came. Again she demanded information on Asa Mercer. This time Harry wrote an immediate reply strong enough to discourage any idea she might have about latching onto any Mercer-inspired journey. When her following missives failed to refer to him, Harry promptly put it out of his mind.

Change had come to the area in other ways. Reverend Clifton returned from the Indian village visibly shaken. He refused to disclose what happened there but a noticeable difference in the next weeks' sermons hinted of a second confrontation with Chief Running Wolf and another verbal defeat. Several times Brian saw the sorry-looking horse cut across the clearing and disappear down the trail. Each time, the same feeling of unease he'd experienced earlier haunted him. For one thing, Clifton seldom stopped by, even when a curl of smoke from the chimney invited and announced the cabin owners were at home. Brian told himself he imagined a furtiveness in the minister's quick glance and the way he prodded the horse into the trail and finally decided to mind his own business.

"A man should be for commending someone who admits he's wrong and goes after folks with the Gospel," he mused. "Mayhap I just don't care for pale-faced preachers." A good-natured grin split his tanned face. "Best I keep in the reverend's good graces. If I ever take me a wife, I'll need him to do the splicing."

The next moment he roared. "Why am I thinking such things, anyway? As if the kind of woman I'd want would look at the likes of a redheaded Irishman like me."

Did Harry sense his friend's thoughts? It seemed so. That night he said with the eagerness to bestow on others the great good fortune he felt had come to him with Alice's love, "I hope you'll help me look after Heather when she comes, Blarney."

"You're her brother. Sure you'll be doing that."

"Uh, she won't want to hang around all the time with Alice and me." His clear skin reddened.

Brian's eyes shone with fun. "Fine thing! Bring your twin thousands of miles from home, then foist her off on a stranger."

"You know I didn't mean that. I just thought you—she—"

"So 'tis matchmaking, you're doing." Brian stared, hiding the fact he'd secretly envisioned the possibility of such a natural outcome of the close living arrangements they'd be sharing. Out of curiosity he asked, "Not that it will happen, but should the good Father ever have it in mind, would you honestly be for trusting Heather, part of yourself, to a rough sailor-logger like me?"

The fire of friendship burned deep in the hazel eyes when Harry simply said, "I could ask no better man in all the world to be my brother, even if I already didn't see him that way."

Brian felt a wave of humility equal to the greatest ocean swells that battered the *Cutlass* wash over him. He wordlessly gripped his friend's hand, sealing the bond between them forever.

With the coming of winter 1865, work slackened. Snow brought a respite to the hardworking loggers. Some drifted into Seattle and picked up what work they could find on the docks and in the various businesses. Others, mostly the married men, and Brian and Harry, used the time to make improvements to their homes. A small community with far-apart neighbors who yet proved available in time of need ringed Reverend Clifton's church in every direction. Emboldened by the wives who made homes in the wilderness, a scattering of other loggers married and new faces dotted the church services.

Long before Christmas, Harry selected his gifts for the two girls he loved so much: beaded moccasins made by Crying Dove at his request. Chief Running Wolf haughtily refused payment for his daughter's work but his eyes glistened when Harry and Brian showed up with a secondhand but well-oiled rifle for him, and a comb and brush set for Crying Dove. "A gift from friends," Harry told them, making it impossible to refuse. "I wish we could have afforded a new rifle."

"Old rifle like good friend," the chief solemnly told him and peered down the barrel.

"Chief, the reverend is having a program on Christmas Eve to honor Jesus, Son of the Great Spirit. Will you come?"

The Indian looked at Harry then at the rifle.

"It has nothing to do with the gifts," Brian hastened to assure him. "Reverend Clifton has learned much and the children will sing. Come if you can. You, too, Crying Dove." He hurried Harry away without forcing the chief to make a commitment. Out of earshot he said, "The look on Running Wolf's face when he thought the rifle was a bribe said a great deal about his dealings with whites."

"Thanks for catching it. I didn't." Harry drew in a deep breath. "Better step it up. It smells like snow. At least, now that we have the horses, it doesn't take so long to get home."

Christmas Eve saw a packed church. After the service, gifts for the children would be given, purchased by donations of all who could spare a little something. The Reverend Clifton had written back East months earlier and every child would receive warm mittens. In addition, small brown paper pokes holding a few pieces of store-bought candy and nuts in the shell lay ready and waiting beneath the spicy fir in the corner of the church, enough for adults as well as children.

In the midst of "Joy to the World" the door swung inward. Chief Running Wolf and Crying Dove had come. This time the joy of Christmas made people crowd together to make room. Brian saw a tinge of color come to the reverend's pale face and he ceremoniously said at the end of the carol, "We are pleased to have Chief Running Wolf and his daughter Crying Dove with us to celebrate the birth of Jesus." He smiled and the chief's face relaxed and Crying Dove's eyes glowed in the candle and lamplight.

Never had Brian been more touched than when the children drilled by the reverend, presented tableaus portraying a night almost 1900 years earlier. The lowing of an unwilling cow participant, the bray of a donkey—both tied outside the window—gave reality, as did the reluctance in the face of the young innkeeper. He did fine with his part, repeating, "There is no room in the inn," but when an even younger Joseph substituted his own lines and said, "That makes me sad," the innkeeper could stand no more.

"There's room in the bunkhouse," he called.

"Thanks. We'll go there." The terse reply sent a ripple through the room but mercifully, the audience held back laughter, even when "Mary" reminded her husband, "We hafta go to the barn or Jesus won't get borned."

Brian risked a glance at the Indian visitors. They sat entranced. Angels with wobbly halos appeared, shepherds in lumberjack coats, one carrying a bleating lamb. Wise Men gloriously aware of their paper crowns. A live baby in a straw-filled wooden packing box, blinking in the dim light and waving a small hand at the world.

"Psst." During the singing of "Silent Night" Harry pulled at Brian's arm. "What are we going to do about the chief and Crying Dove? They can have our candy sacks but shouldn't they get gifts?"

"It will be all right," Brian whispered back. "The mittens are only for the children."

Harry relaxed. Reverend Clifton gave a short message, urging his hearers to remember Jesus didn't always stay a baby but grew up and died on the cross that all might be saved. What a far cry from his first sermon in the little church!

Candle stubs securely fastened to the tree were lit. Men with buckets of water stayed nearby just in case. Child after child went forward to receive a brown paper package, each showing excitement, from the gap-toothed young boy to the toddler.

Brian looked at the chief and pity filled him. The Indian's face worked and his dark gaze never left the children. Were his thoughts on those in his tribe, children who perhaps had no mittens for warmth? Volunteers passed out the sacks of candy and nuts. Chief Running Wolf accepted his with a nod. Then Reverend Clifton, who had responded with a quick glance at the chief in answer to Brian's pointed stare and indicating head said, "We have several pairs of mittens left. Chief Running Wolf, you will do us a favor if you take them to your village."

The chief rose. So did Crying Wolf. "I will take." He waited until Clifton bundled them into an awkward bundle and brought them to him. Crying Dove immediately took the parcel, smiled a smile of singular sweetness at the young minister and followed her father out into the night. Neither had caught a little byplay Brian's sharp eyes detected; two of the loggers' wives who had a passel of children between them had quietly slipped in the mittens their youngsters laid aside.

Brian's eyes stung. He knew only too well the extent of the sacrifice. He had seen such happenings in Ireland, the poor sharing with those even less fortunate. He thought of the kindly neighbor and her son in Cork and how after a long time he kept his promise and wrote to them, enclosing a bit of money; of their grateful answer that followed him for months and finally caught up with the *Cutlass*.

None of the sacrifices equal what Jesus did.

Brian jerked erect. Had someone spoken? No, around him adults visited and children shouted with enjoyment. He shrugged off the sense of something unfinished that twanged against his soul. Something he had heard so long ago he couldn't even remember who said it came to mind. "You'll never get the blessed Savior off your mind until you invite Him into your soul." Surrounded by the rude trappings of a makeshift Bethlehem, the lad within the man he had become trembled. One day he must face his Maker. Would it be as the brash sailor who fought to make his way? Or as one who bowed head, heart, and knee before the King, claiming forgiveness through His Son?

Sobered by the thoughts he couldn't keep from coming, Brian Boru O'Rourke, named for a mighty king, silently helped clear away the remains of the evening.

Reverend Clifton spoke in his ear. "I don't understand it. I counted and counted and there were just enough mittens for the white children." He looked honestly puzzled.

Brian started to explain, stopped when he caught the look of disapproval and headshake of one of the generous mothers. He quickly said, "Aren't you for preaching the miracle of the loaves and fishes? Why question? Just be glad the Indian children—at least some of them—will have warm hands and know we cared. You did well, Reverend, to make it appear Chief Running Wolf would be doing us the favor. He's a proud man."

"I know." Clifton stopped what he was doing. "Sometimes I wish. . ."

Brian never knew what the minister wished. Someone called for him to explain where things went and he walked away. Yet a certain something in the minister's face left the redheaded man feeling more kindly toward Clifton than he had before.

Shortly after Christmas, a disturbing letter arrived from Alice. It nearly drove Harry to distraction. He paced the floor of their snug home and raged. "She hasn't gotten the idea of Mercer out of her head," he shouted. "After all I told her! Why doesn't she listen?" He raked his fingers through his brown hair until he resembled pictures of headhunters.

"Better send her a letter right away," Brian advised and went back to the sketch he'd begun of his new home. He could barely wait for spring. He'd trade winter fog for the gray of pussy willows and sound of peepers singing from the frog ponds any time. Restlessness at being kept inside by an icy storm that swept across the Sound made little things appear big.

He tried to tell that to Harry but his friend said, "You just don't know Alice Freeman. She should have been named Freewoman. She's stubborn as a mule, and doggone it, I wouldn't change her." He grinned sheepishly and headed for writing materials. "Well, not much."

Brian chuckled and wondered for the hundredth time how fair Alice and sheltered Heather would fit in Washington Territory.

six

The frantic letter Harry Templeton wrote insisting that Alice and Heather put away forever any idea of joining the Mercer expedition sped its way toward the East Coast. At the same time, the young women rushed headlong into preparations. To Heather's surprise, the usually heedless Alice settled into the deviousness to accomplish their Herculean task. List after list plotted their escape, everything from how to get their trunks away without family interference to the letters to be posted at the last possible moment.

"We must not be stopped." Alice's round eyes had never looked bluer or more determined.

A poignant look of renunciation swept into Heather's' heart. "No." She didn't need to add her need to get away. Alice knew only too well how thin the ice, how deep the lake of Adelaide Templeton's hatred. She squeezed her friend's hand.

"We'll be gone long before the time is up. Your father said you had a month. By then you'll be beyond his reach."

"And hers." Heather pressed her lips together. Even to Alice, so excited and filled with anticipation of seeing Harry again, his twin could not express how torn she felt. Years of suppressed bitterness, intense love for her father, and guilt because she felt her Christian witness to Adelaide should somehow make things bet-

ter had led to the final act of rebellion but it still was
not easy.

"The *Continental* isn't taking nearly as many girls
as Mr. Mercer hoped." Alice broke into Heather's dark
thoughts. She tossed her flaxen curls. "Not that I care."
She giggled. "I heard most of those going are widows, middle class, and respectable. When people dared
cast reflections on their morals and label them husband hunters they just stuck their noses in the air and
left the gossipmongers with their tittle-tattle."

"I still have some misgivings. Harry is going to be
wild when he learns what we've done. As for Father
. . ." She couldn't finish the sentence.

"Mama and Daddy will rave and rant, then shake
their heads over their wayward daughter and be secretly proud," Alice said complacently. "Mama ran
away from home to marry and she was two years
younger than I am now."

"One good thing," Heather mused. "I'll be twenty-
one on June first and I understand it will take almost
until then to reach Seattle. Once I get safely away, Father and Adelaide won't be able to do anything about
it. Not that she will want to. It will give her more
proof of how awful Harry and I are." Hot tears poured
and she choked out, "If I didn't have Harry and you,
I'd be no better than an orphan."

"You have God, too," Alice quietly reminded her.
At times the younger girl surprised Heather with her
insight. Now she flung her arms around her and said,
"Someday, somehow, things will be made right. Until
then, we just have to keep trusting."

Keep trusting. The two words became a talisman and Heather clung to them with all her heart during the days that dwindled to hours before the *Continental* sailed. With the help of a willing but tearstained Katie and supported by the entire staff of servants who were appalled but understanding of her flight, Heather smuggled her trunk out. Most of the servants had already expressed their intention to find other positions once Heather took what little brightness remained in the Templeton home with her. "Let Mrs. sack us," Katie had muttered, folding clothes with a vengeance. "She'll have a time getting anyone else." Fresh tears fell. "If I weren't already promised, I'd go with you."

"I don't know how to explain my absence without lying," Heather worried aloud to Alice and the little maid.

"Simple. We each just have the servants tell our family we're with each other. It's perfectly true. Just thank God your father hasn't forbidden you to leave the house. These bothersome skirts make it hard if I had to pull you out a window and down a ladder!"

Her nonsense lightened their mood and banished one more obstacle.

The night of January 15, 1866, Heather and Alice stayed overnight at the Lovejoy's Hotel, where a number of the Mercer girls had been marking time until the thrilling moment of boarding came. Subdued by the magnitude of their daring, they mingled with the crowd, said little, and received some reassurance from the smiling faces that surrounded them. An air of gaiety prevailed, in sharp contrast with Heather's aching heart and Alice's unusual quiet. The next morning they rose, hastily prepared for the day and eagerly listened to the news that all was well; they would indeed sail that day. Trunks and band boxes filled the express wagon and made the trip more final. One by one the girls and women climbed into coaches and rode through the city streets to the *Continental*, berthed at pier 2, North River.

"Will we never *go*?" Heather shredded her dainty handkerchief with nervous fingers. The time between boarding and sailing felt like an eternity. Any minute Heather expected her father to appear and snatch her away from Alice. If it happened, it meant the institution. Her attempted flight could not be forgiven. How Adelaide would gloat.

Alice, pale-faced but resolute, patted Heather's gloved hand. "It's almost time. Listen."

A cacophony of cries, whistles, clanging bells, and shouts preceded the movement. The *Continental* slowly sailed into the river and on down into the bay.

The wave of relief she experienced threatened to swamp Heather. With each passing hour, her sense of freedom grew. Behind lay imprisonment. Ahead lay Harry, a new life. "God, thank You," she whispered. "I—"

A nearby altercation cut into her prayer. "I tell you, it's true," a low but vehement voice hissed. "The rumor is all over the ship. There are persons on board whose passage is not paid for."

"You mean Mercer didn't take care of it?" a horrified female voice exclaimed.

"Shhh. I don't know anything except that some on this very ship are going to be sent back when we come to anchor off quarantine—Staten Island. I heard that every ticket will be examined and those who draw a blank will be refused passage."

Heather felt the blood drain from her face. Alice clutched at her for support. "What if it's *us*?" She looked like a snow girl with frightened blue eyes and a lock of flaxen hair escaping from beneath her hat.

"I can't go back. I'll have to run away, find work, anything. Alice, *I can't go back.*"

A look came to her friend's face, one Heather knew she would remember forever. "If one of us is forced to abandon the journey, it must not be you. Harry and his friend will send passage money soon and I'll come." Desolation colored her voice but she bravely kept her chin high.

"I wouldn't have dared come if it hadn't been for you," Heather reminded.

"It doesn't matter. Mama and Daddy will be so glad I didn't go now they are sure to let me sail when the money comes," Alice comforted. "Even if they don't, you cannot be sent back."

Heather didn't know what to do. *Keep trusting.* She spoke the words aloud. "Keep trusting, Alice."

"I will."

Hearts fearful, the passengers, all of whom had heard the unpleasant rumors, gathered in groups, all bearing the same question, spoken or unspoken, "Who will be sent back? Will it be I?" A little ripple of fear ran through the crowd when the *Continental* anchored and passengers received orders to meet in the lower saloon. Heather found the suspense almost unendurable as each person was called to have his or her ticket inspected. Alice stumbled away, came back with a look

of gladness that changed to misery. "Mine is paid."
The expressions of anger and loud cries from those
who didn't pass inspection rent Heather's heart. What
if she were to be one of them? Could she bear to take
Alice's ticket? Would she even be allowed to do so?
If not, only God could care for her.

"Miss Heather Templeton." In fear and trembling,
she answered the call, produced her ticket and waited.
It felt like hours passed before the official gruffly said,
"In order." She never knew how she got back to Alice
through the blinding mist in front of her eyes, too dazed
to even give thanks. Not until Alice's face lighted could
Heather fully realize she was still part of the Mercer
expedition.

"I feel so sorry for them," tenderhearted Alice sobbed
when two families and sixteen girls were ordered to
gather their things. Heather shivered and watched them.

"There, but for God's mercy, are we," she reminded.
The rejected ones were herded onto the tug boat alongside. Snatches of stories by those who had given up
everything floated in the air. A Mr. Conant, of the
New York Times, could do little, although passengers
called on him for protection, should the *Continental*
sail without Asa Mercer, who had been strangely missing during the loading. "Please, for the love of God,
don't send us back," two young girls pleaded. "We're
orphans. We put ourselves in Mercer's care."

"Mercer said you had to go," they were told.

"No. No. We have no money. We will die."

Heather took a step forward. "Alice, I can't stand
this. One of them can have my place."

Alice stared at her, then at the young orphans. Her

face twisted. "And mine."

Before they could arrange the exchange of their tickets for the worthless ones, a man called, "Wait. I will pay their passage." He produced the fare and the girls fell weeping at his feet. "Here, there. Stop that. Don't thank me. My sister, Miss Mary Bermingham, felt sorry for you." He looked embarrassed and managed to free himself and stride off.

The depths of Heather's gratefulness toward the kindly Miss Bermingham knew no bound. Yet while the two had been saved from being banished, the tug pulled away with the others who still hurled threats toward Asa Mercer. Danger had passed and Heather whirled when a smiling girl beckoned two of the men.

"Remove the hatches from the coal hole," she told them. Once it had been done, the girl leaned down. "Come out, Mr. Mercer. They've gone." Never had there been a sorrier-looking sight than the cowardly Mercer, streaked with coal dust, who forced others to tell those who had in good faith signed for passage they would be returned to New York.

Spirits rose and Alice, especially, ate heavily of the excellent meal served early the next morning but Heather picked at her food. The release of knowing she had actually escaped her stepmother's torture and her father's threats left her exhausted. Freezing weather had made staterooms cozy and welcoming early the previous night but she'd tossed and turned, unaccustomed to a new bed. Heavy-eyed and still tired, she awakened to the sound of chattering and running feet. All Heather wanted to do was go back to sleep, with the tiny heather planting she'd smuggled aboard nearby.

By nine, the *Continental* raised anchor and sailed. Alas for Alice and those who had stuffed themselves at breakfast, seasickness swept through the ranks and kept those who escaped it busy helping the less fortunate. Alice had one of the sharpest attacks but also the best nurse. Heather roused from her lethargy and cared for her, wiping the hot forehead with cool cloths. A choppy sea that night made things worse and the pitching of the ship left most of those aboard terrified and calling on Mercer for help he could not give.

Heather simply talked to her Heavenly Father and cared for Alice. No storm at sea could be any more frightening than the prospects that lay behind her. Besides, she marveled, hadn't the Master calmed the sea with a few words? Out on the ocean in the midst of a gale, peace she hadn't felt since her mother died stole into her heart and quieted her fears.

The sickness continued for several days but at last the time came when Alice, assisted by Heather, shakily made her way to deck for fresh air. For the first time, they learned more of the ship and her crew, including Captain Winser, an excellent seaman, respected by all. A feeling of assurance came into Heather's heart when she saw the kindly captain, who had brought his wife and seventeen-year-old daughter Minnie with him. She soon became friends with Alice and Heather, and her frank, fun-loving personality provided hours of enjoyment.

On Sunday, Asa Mercer held services in the upper saloon, but neither Heather nor Alice attended, being in secret agreement with outspoken Miss Mary Bermingham, champion of the two orphan girls, who branded Mercer a hypocrite in preaching what he hadn't practiced. Those who did, reported he had instead read one of Henry Ward Beecher's sermons. The girls quietly read their Bibles and prayed together in a deserted corner of the deck. Despite the variety of persons aboard ship, they preferred one another's company for the most part and never tired of talking about Washington Territory, Harry, and the red-headed Irishman, Brian O'Rourke.

"He will fall in love with you," Alice predicted, her gaze turned westward.

"Don't be silly." Heather glanced up from a blouse she had brought topside to mend, taking advantage of the pleasant afternoon.

"I'm not. Any man would fall in love with you. I'm glad Harry's your twin or I wouldn't have a chance."

Heather threw her head back and laughed. "As if Harry has ever looked at any girl but you or ever will!"

"I know. Isn't it wonderful?" Alice, who had fully recovered from her initial bout with illness, had proved to be as good a sailor as Heather. Now she bounced a bit and shifted to look at her friend. "We're the lucky ones. I can't even remember a time I didn't know someday I'd marry Harry."

The mending lay still in Heather's lap. "I don't know what it's like to have such feelings. Is that why you were willing to leave everything and everyone?"

"Yes. Someday you will be, too."

With the gentle swell of a friendly blue sea meeting blue sky and the ship noises that had become so familiar Heather scarcely noticed them, their friendship had deepened in the days since they sailed.

Yet the sea did not always remain friendly. The loss of a man who fell overboard and drowned saddened the expedition. Storms came that tossed the ship as a boy tosses a ball. The resulting sickness dampened moods, although every day took them farther from New York and closer to the journey's end that felt like a far off dream, perhaps never to be realized.

Stories of Mr. Mercer's proposing to one of the company swelled in humor and absurdity each time repeated. Heather and Alice stayed apart from the young officers who clearly showed they would welcome a flirtation. Not all the girls did the same and on moonlight nights, couples dotted the deck. Heather scorned those who allowed arms about their waists, yet a longing for a day when she would know love slipped into her soul, despite its *no trespassing* sign. She blushed at Alice's innocent teasing but finally said, "Please don't. I'll be self-conscious when I meet Mr. O'Rourke."

Alice subsided and peace prevailed.

February second brought an experience none would forget. Heather, Alice and the others crowded the decks in response to the shout, "Come and see."

"What is it?"

"The Southern Cross."

Heather tightened her fingers on the rail and gasped. A navy-velvet sky like an inverted bowl hovered over the *Continental*. Stars clustered, resembling silver flowers close enough to pick. She turned her head and a flood of sheer beauty flowed through her. The constellation she had only heard about hung in the sky as if suspended on a string. Its perfect crossbar of space

shimmered in the heavens, a symbol of hope to weary
travelers, the way the Cross at Calvary offered hope
and salvation. The four glittering stars lit the southern
hemisphere with a beauty sublime, indescribable, never
to be forgotten by those who gazed with eager hearts
as well as watching eyes.

Once across the Equator, excitement built. "It seems
so-so foreign," Alice said and Heather heartily agreed
with her, even more so when they approached Rio de
Janeiro's gorgeous harbor with its rising Serra Dos
Orgos range on one side and rocky islands in the sea
on the other. Steep Sugar Loaf Mountain and green
wooded hills offered relief from the endless ocean's
waters. A trip into the city with Captain Winser brought
mixed sights: Negro slaves bare from the waist up,
narrow streets, mule-drawn hacks, antiquity beyond
belief, turbaned women, a large fountain said to be
used as a public wash basin, strange and highly-col-
ored birds. In spite of the sights, however, Heather
and Alice secretly rejoiced when the *Constitution* once
more sailed.

Names and places known only from books became
real to the passengers. The Straits of Magellan, cold,
chilly, windy. Patagonia, side wheel ducks, balmy as
June in spite of the early March date. The Pacific, vastly
different from the Atlantic—peaceful by name, if not
always by whim. The Galapagos Islands, lava and
cactus adorned, a chance for Heather, Alice and the
others to discard shoes and stockings and wade in the
water.

At last, April 24th. The *Continental* sailed through
the Golden Gate Channel, past Alcatraz Island and into

San Francisco. Heather looked at the forbidding buildings and shivered. It had been used as a military barracks during the War. How could anyone bear to live there? Ever since her father had threatened to institutionalize her, Heather found herself unable to stand the thought of caged or isolated persons.

So near and yet so far! The girls tearfully said goodbye to those who listened to stories of Washington Territory's crude conditions and decided to stay in San Francisco. Alice and Heather impatiently waited for Mercer to arrange passage to Puget Sound on lumber vessels. On May 1st they boarded the *Scotland* and headed north on the last stage of their long journey, with about half those who stayed fast to the Washington Territory dream. Over and over Alice exclaimed, "Just a few days more." The closer they got to Seattle, the more she bubbled, thriving as Heather's namesake twig had done.

Heather reacted the other way. There had been a certain security aboard the *Continental*, with all its tossings, but ever since stepping ashore at San Francisco, strange feelings cropped up within her, fears Alice pooh-poohed.

"Everything will be wonderful, just wait and see," the intrepid girl predicted. Not until the day arrived when they would dock in Seattle did she lose her calm. Heather found her friend staring in the mirror, eyes wet.

"Whatever is the matter?" she demanded.

"Wh-what if he doesn't love me after all? Wh-what if he thinks I'm not as pretty as he remembers or—"

"'O ye of little faith,'" Heather quoted. "What do

you think Harry will do? Say, 'Begone, woman. I may
have slaved to raise passage money, been saved all of
it by your escapade and prayed day and night since
your letter came months ago, but I've changed my
mind'?"

"N-no." Alice laughed and swiped at her eyes child-
ishly. "Oh, dear, I'm a perfect fright."

Heather lost her own feeling of strangeness in comforting the suddenly fearful Alice, who clung like a
limpet and proved worthless in assembling their bag-
gage.

Their first sight of Seattle proved glorious and dis-
appointing. Glorious when they raised their gaze toward Mount Rainier, looked over Puget Sound, and
noticed the forests that pointed to the sky. Disappoint-
ing because of the settlement itself, the sawdust streets,
the many grogshops.

Alice gasped and Heather automatically tried to cheer
her. "Remember, Harry doesn't live here. His cabin is
out in the woods near where he works." Her heart
thumped at the idea and she frankly admitted Seattle
didn't meet expectation. On the other hand, neither did
it appear to be as raw and crude as Asa Mercer had
made out. Perhaps he hadn't wanted to build false hopes
but the more she looked, the more Heather realized
this city might be uncivilized but the majestic setting's
beauty appealed to something in her, formerly un-
touched.

"Where's Harry?" Alice stood on tiptoe, straining to
see through the crowd that had come to meet the ves-
sel. A moment later her high, sweet voice rang above
the din. "There he is!"

Heather stretched to see. Her gaze followed Alice's pointing finger. Could that be her twin, that tall, filled-out man with sun-bleached brown hair and a deeply tanned face? A lump composed of equal parts of joy and relief cut off any greeting she could make. Her vision blurred. She dashed away the mist. Whatever lay behind her was gone forever. Her new life began now, here in Washington Territory. She must not face it—or Harry—with sadness and tears.

Heather raised her chin, followed Alice from the ship and irrelevantly wondered why Brian O'Rourke had not also come to meet them. No flaming red head stood out in the crowd.

seven

The instant Harry got Alice's hastily scribbled letter posted just before the girls boarded the *Continental*, he knew his order for her to forget such a mad scheme had failed to reach her. "Not that I'd put it past her to come anyway," he ruefully told Brian. "It's just that my letter wouldn't have had time to arrive in New York."

"So by now she and your sister are on the high seas." Why should a thrill go through the Irishman? Quick memories of days and nights on the ocean flipped through his mind and whispered the answer. Although he had been contented enough since he turned landlubber, his long years with Captain Haines on the *Cutlass* would never be forgotten. "Well, they'll be for having adventures."

"Storms and seasickness and boredom," Harry grunted in a departure from his usual self.

"Sure. And sunrises and sunsets, foreign shores and curiosities the like of which aren't seen in America."

Harry forgot his glooms. His hazel eyes gleamed. "Do you ever regret leaving it?"

Brian shook his head. "No. For I found a brother." In the stillness created by his solemn vow, Harry awkwardly reached out and gripped the other's hand.

"It was bad enough waiting for spring before," he complained a few minutes later. "Now, it's worse."

He straightened. "What if one of the ship's officers snags Alice? She's pretty enough to have any of them she wants."

"She always has been, according to you, so why worry now?"

The younger man's troubled look fled. "I don't know what I'd do without you."

"We'd best be thinking about all the things we have to get done several months earlier than expected," Brian reminded him. "Once the woods open up in the spring and we start putting in a garden and building the O'Rourke Palace, there'll be no time for the building of furniture."

Goaded by his comment, the two men spent every waking hour turning the cabin into a solid, comfortable home. At times while working with his cheery, whistling companion, Brian envied the lad. A home, his Alice coming, health and strength. What more could a man ask? He also wistfully envied Harry's trust in God. Where Brian believed, mainly due to Captain Haines and his teachings, Harry knew God in a personal way that often left the former sailor speechless. Their hours working together offered endless opportunities for discussion and Harry never lost a chance to point out how God worked in His children's lives. Brian argued from the standpoint of one whose family had not seemingly been blessed of God. "What kind of God lets famine come, while rich men fill their bellies?" he demanded.

Harry's eyes glistened. "Would you have God treat people as marionettes?" he shot back. "Poor creatures to move and dance only when the strings are pulled?

God gave agency, Blarney. Even when people choose wrong and it hurts Him, He allows it."

"Seems He'd make folks do better. I would, if I were God."

Harry sadly shook his head. "He wants us to serve Him because we choose to, not because we're forced to." He paused, then added, "Tell me now, when you were on the *Cutlass*, to whom did men give their best? The man who beat them or the one they admired and respected?"

Brian thought of Captain Haines, who had never lifted his hand against the boy who made mistakes, but painstakingly instructed him so he'd do it right the next time. A glimmer of understanding seeped into his heart and mind, and he turned away without answering.

January passed. Then February. March rained in and the two who waited found themselves busier than ever. Newspaper reports of the *Continental*'s journey continued to headline and contend for and against Mercer and his expedition. April arrived smiling and blooming, pointing out its advantage over stormy March. By the end of the month, an unfinished but picturesque cabin snuggled into the northwest corner of Harry Templeton's land as if it had been there forever. Only the newness of the logs betrayed its recent origin. From the front, a never-ending view of Mount Rainier and the rising sun offered splendor to feed a man's soul. Or a woman's. Brian grinned to himself. The building of his cabin had naturally resulted in thoughts of a companion. He could be happy here forever with the right wife.

"How's a man to know who the right one is?" he complained to Harry late one evening when they wearily trudged home after a few hours work on the cabin in the newly-cleared spot.

Rosy streaks from the setting sun colored his friend's face. A look of unutterable sweetness came. "No one can tell you how. You'll just know."

"A lot of help you're for being, I don't think."

Harry dealt him a blow on the shoulder and grinned like an imp bent on mischief. "Sure, and who could be resisting the Blarney Castle, even if a gurrrl has to be taking you with it?" He laughed and the sound echoed in the evening hush.

"Fine name for a man's home," Brian grumbled but a matching grin showed even white teeth. "You'd think Miller and the rest of the crew would have more respect for the Ould Sod. Some of them have Irish ancestors."

"Don't be a jackass," Harry told him. "Think they'd be over here spending their precious time off helping if they didn't admire and respect you? Besides, you couldn't have given it a better name if you'd thought for—" He broke off and stared. "Why, isn't that Reverend Clifton? Wonder what he's doing at our cabin this time of day?" They quickened their steps.

The white-faced man who never tanned no matter how much time he spent outdoors turned from the door at their steps, hand still upraised to knock. His sad horse drooped by the porch. A feeling of something amiss sent qualms through Brian. Never had he seen the minister so distraught. In the months since his first sermon he had grown much more human and his preaching reflected humility and not just the law.

"Templeton, O'Rourke. Thank God you're here!" With long strides he leaped to the ground and came toward them, hands held out in a groping gesture.

"What's wrong?" Harry demanded.

Clifton licked his lips and his voice sounded husky, "I have to go."

"Go? Go where?"

Brian's mind echoed the question.

"Back East, at least for a time. I received word my mother is terribly ill. I just pray she will be there by the time I arrive." He wrung his hands and anguish contorted his features. "This is such a bad time for me to leave, I scarcely know what to do."

Brian dropped a comforting arm over the shaking shoulders. "Faith, and your church will be fine, Reverend. If we can't be for finding a preacher, Harry here will conduct services."

Clifton just shook his head. "You don't understand. You can't."

Poor chap, Brian thought. He's that close to his mother he can't bear the thought of her being taken.

Harry's face wrinkled in compassion. "God will care for you and bring you safely back to us in His time," he said.

Reverend Clifton just stared at him then, he laughed, a hollow sound that sent shivers through Brian. "Time? Oh, yes, time. That's funny, isn't it?" He dropped his head to his hands and laughed that croaking laugh again.

The other two men managed to get him in the house and urged him to drink the strong coffee they brewed and eat the cold cornbread and a piece of meat left over from supper. Harry invited him to stay overnight but he said he could not. He must leave early the next morning on the first available ship.

"Do you have passage money?" Brian asked.

He nodded but the faraway look in his eyes showed he barely heard the question. Brian had the feeling something lurked behind his lips, needing to be said but unable to come out. Reverend Clifton at last mounted his sorry steed, sighed and straightened in the saddle. "Tell—Running Wolf I had to go. We have become friends." The pale face gleamed in the dusk and the words came just above a whisper. "Tell him I will be back, no matter what. Promise me you'll do that."

"Of course. God bless." Brian and Harry waved until the figure dimmed and disappeared before turning back into the house.

"I wouldn't have figured him to care what the Chief thought when he first came," Harry observed. He lit a lamp and its yellow flame shone through the polished globe and brightened the room, driving away shadows. "Just goes to show what this Washington Territory can do for a man. Couldn't help feeling sorry for him. I know how it felt to lose my mother."

"So do I." Brian started to comment on the minister's strange laugh and thought better of it. Folks acted different when faced with crisis situations. Why fault Clifton for his unusual behavior? "I wonder if we can get a new preacher?" he continued. "Should be able to, with the church and all."

Harry drew himself up in mock dignity. His nose went into the air and he turned the corners of his laughing mouth down. "Well! And after you were the one who suggested that I take over. You've reconsidered, I see."

"Don't be a jackass," Brian told him in the exact tone Harry had used earlier. "You can preach better than he can. I should know. You're for practicing on me enough." He dodged Harry's good-natured blow and headed for soap and water to wash away the good sweat earned from work on the Blarney Castle.

The next Sunday morning Harry acquitted himself so well during the morning service, the members unanimously voted not to replace Reverend Clifton if young Templeton would agree to fill in. A weathered logger known for his dedication to his Lord put it succinctly. "Rev. Clifton got so he suited us fine. If a new parson comes, we have to jump in and start all over, trainin' him, you might say."

"But I have my logging job and am busy building," Harry protested.

"Think on it, son. It's your chance to do somethin' for your Maker." He turned to the little group of loggers who had come to hear "the kid" preach. "If Templeton here takes over as preacher, just for Sundays—we ain't expectin' him to do all the visitin' Rev. Clifton did—will you come?"

Miller scratched his head and cocked an eyebrow. "Maybe." Some of the others grunted but grinned. Brian had the feeling they'd support Harry.

"Why don't you do it, Blarney?" Harry impulsively said. "You're the one with the gift of gab."

Brian flashed back, "I'm not for being a preacher but I'll lick the first mick who says a word against you!"

Gasps from the more righteous mingled with haw-haws from the others and before they left, Harry had agreed to give it a try, but with the understanding that if at any time either he or the congregation had second thoughts, another man would be found and no hard feelings on either side.

On the way home, he shook his head. "I can't believe I agreed to such a thing."

Brian ducked to avoid a low hanging branch over the trail. "Just think how proud Alice will be to become a preacher's wife."

"I'm not a preacher," Harry automatically retorted before he smirked and said, "Just think how impressed my sister would be if she arrived and found you in the pulpit." He touched heels to his horse's sides and the animal danced out of Brian's reach.

That afternoon Brian reminded, "We haven't given Chief Running Wolf the reverend's message yet. It's a beautiful day. Let's ride to the village."

"Good idea."

It didn't take long to saddle the horses and head down the trail, into the forest, and reach the bluff above the Indian camp. Now the well-used path little resembled the faintly-marked way they'd ridden the summer before. The chief and his daughter used it when they occasionally came to church and on their even more rare visits to the cabin in the clearing. Reverend Clifton had ridden it often. Yet just as many birds twittered and depending on the time of day, deer, a coyote now and then, even a red fox sometimes crossed their path.

Chief Running Wolf's taciturn face twitched in what went for a smile and the midnight-black eyes brightened.

"Sorry we've been so long coming, Chief," Harry breezily told him. "We're working on the place and new cabin most of the daylight hours when we aren't in the woods."

Chief Running Wolf nodded and crossed his arms over his chest. Brian saw the women drying fish and busy at their tasks, only half listening while Harry gave the chief Reverend Clifton's message.

"He said to tell you he'd be back, no matter what. He acted all broken up about it. The reverend must love his mother a great deal."

Something in Chief Running Wolf's rigid stance jerked Brian's attention back and he heard the Indian say, "So he is gone." The Irishman couldn't tell if the words held relief or contempt. Did the friendship Clifton claimed exist only in the minister's mind? Perhaps in some way he had offended the chief.

"Who is gone, Father?" Lovely Crying Dove had slipped to where they stood, soft-moccasined feet making no sound.

"I was just telling your father that Reverend Clifton's mother is very ill and he had to go to her."

"He is gone?" A flicker came and went in Crying Dove's dark eyes. Brian knew it had been there despite its flight. His blue gaze, sharpened by years of watching at sea, also noticed a quick trembling of her lips that stilled immediately and he knew. Crying Dove had been attracted to Clifton. It explained Chief Running Wolf's response to the news. The subject changed but Brian could not forget the incident. Just as well the minister had been called away. Crying Dove's beauty couldn't help but appeal to many men but a match be-

tween the Indian princess and Reverend Clifton would
be impossible. Even if he ever learned to love her and
married her, it meant the end of his ministerial career.
Those who in the spirit of Christmas and the Babe in
the manger had accepted their dark-skinned visitors
would not stand for a squawman minister. Brian sighed.
Strange the good Lord would create so many different
races who squabbled and fought and despised one another. But then, hadn't Jesus been despised, too, for
His humble birth to a Jewish peasant girl? He shook
his curly head and decided to leave theological discus-
sions to those more qualified.

Like wildfire the news chased north. The *Continental* had sailed through Golden Gate Channel! Mercer
and his girls were in San Francisco and some of them
planned to stay.

"Not our girls," Harry said a dozen times, gaze turned
south. "It's just a matter of time. Whew, let's stop a
minute."

Brian obligingly let go of his end of the crosscut
saw and wiped sweat from his face after shaking sawdust from his heavy work gloves. He and Harry made
a fine team and their daily showing equaled that of
more experienced loggers. The bull of the woods didn't
come out and say so but the squint in his eyes and
quickly smothered grin betrayed his satisfaction.

"Hey, Blarney," Miller bellowed. "You better make
a good first impression before Miss Heather sees me
or you won't have a chance."

"The biggest impression you make is when you're
for hitting someone with that hard head of yours," Brian
hollered back but Miller just laughed and went on with

his work.

The Blarney Castle stood finished and ready. That night Brian transferred his belongings to it. A pang went through him when he remembered the long winter days and evenings of sharing.

Harry must have been feeling the same way for he quietly said, "I'm getting a wife but she won't have the same place you have. Nothing can change our brotherhood. I know you'd stand by me if no one on earth believed in me."

"And you'd be for doing the same."

"You're going with me to meet them," Harry added. Mischief danced in his hazel eyes. "Can't let Heather see Miller's ugly mug first. Remember what he said."

"He's going to be there? How? For that matter, how will you know which boat they'll be taking?"

"Got a message from Alice written just before they boarded the *Scotland*. No, Miller won't be there, but you can bet he will scout around, maybe even pull some shenanigan such as meeting our buggy—should say, our borrowed buggy. Glad the straw boss said we could use it, although later we'll probably have to take a team and wagon in to haul trunks and the like."

Brian considered. "I'm for thinking if I were a young lady who had sailed thousands of miles to reach my sweetheart or even my brother, I'd not be wanting a stranger present."

"Stranger!" Harry glared at him. "Who's been using his wages and inheritance to fix up a place? Who's worked until he was ready to drop so things would be nice and not too rough for Eastern ladies? Man, if you're a stranger, I'll give away friends and start welcoming any unknown man who comes to my door." Like dandelion puff that sails away with a change of wind, his mood lightened. "The Bible talks about strangers maybe being angels." He cocked his head. "I never heard of an angel who needed a shave but—"

"For the love of Mike, will you stop blathering? So I'm not a stranger. I still think these colleens have the right to get acquainted with all that's new and different a little at a time. I'd rather be here waiting with a plume of smoke curling from your cabin, the door open wide, maybe some wildflowers stuck in a jar. Just picture yourself driving all those miles on the rutted road, through the forest with glimpses of the Sound sometimes showing. You come to the turn, take our trail that's now a road, thanks to hard work and sweat. The horses quicken their pace, knowing home's for being just ahead. The buggy rolls out of the woods, across the clearing, past the garden we put in, also with hard work and sweat."

Harry sat with eyes half-closed, mesmerized by the beguiling Irish-poetry description.

Brian's voice took on a croon. "You lift Miss Alice down. Then Miss Heather. The smell of good venison roast and potatoes baked in the ashes wafts out the open door, along with the cinnamon tang of fresh apple pie—"

"Hold it!" Harry destroyed the enticing atmosphere. "I can't bake pies and neither can you."

"The camp cook can and he already said he'd be for providing dessert for our esteemed visitors," Brian loftily told him. His blue eyes sparkled. "I can do the roast and vegetables." He fixed a not-so-stern gaze on

Harry. "Now, just supposing I were to go with you. No smoke from the chimney. No open, welcoming door. Nor roast or vegetable or pie 'cause I wouldn't be here to get it while it was fresh and the cook informed me either it be fresh or he wouldn't send one."

"Blarney O'Rourke, you're hopeless. You win." Harry flung his hands in the air. "Just one thing." He dropped both hands and placed them on his hips. "If you have any idea of ducking out when you see us coming, forget it. The table had better be set for four and the fourth one isn't to be Miller or anyone but you. Otherwise I'll-I'll—"

"You'll be for having a peeling off my hide the way we peeled poles to make a fence around our garden."

Perversely, once the matter had been settled, when Harry left to meet the *Scotland*, regret filled the older man. Why had he been so stubborn, even with all the valid reasons he had given for not going into Seattle? Seeing the ship come in and the crowd that waited would be better than a dog and pony show. Brian found himself moping and sharply snapped himself up. He and Harry had decided the entourage should spend the night in town and drive out the next day. In the meantime, a final coverlet straightening, sweeping job, and a dozen other things demanded his attention.

"I once heard someone call certain work a labor of love," Brian soliloquized. "Faith, and the building of this home in the wilderness must be just that."

In the early May evening, he stood in the open doorway and surveyed his handiwork. A bouquet of fireweed gathered from a logged-off area loomed rosy in a fruit jar scrubbed until it glistened. The venison roast sizzled in its pan. Not a speck of dust marred the mantel. The table, laid for four, invited weary, hungry travelers. The bearskin rug on the newly-cleaned floor crouched straight and soft. Even the curtains looked perkier than usual, due to a recent washing before going back up alongside polished windows. Two golden-crusted apple pies fresh from the cook shack tempted.

The sound of buggy wheels and a clear, "Halloo, Blarney," sent him to the porch, anticipation darkening his blue eyes and curving his lips in a smile of genuine welcome.

eight

Heather never forgot her first sight of the cabin in the clearing. Clutching the plant she'd carefully tended on the long voyage and with Alice's exclamations of pleasure ringing in her ears, a feeling of contentment filled her. Although she had enjoyed supper the night before at the Occidental, a sigh of relief and feeling of escape came when they left Seattle behind. So many curious onlookers, not all friendly, had made her feel that each time she walked down the street, she ran a gauntlet. Rude comments from a few of the uncouth louts further disturbed her. "No fair getting two of 'em," a man called raucously. It had taken Heather and Alice's combined efforts to keep Harry from wading in and starting what he said his friend Brian would call a donnybrook.

"We're not merchandise," heedless Alice yelled. Heather couldn't decide if the laugh that followed reflected support for her audacity or disbelief. She heartily agreed when Alice sniffed and said, "Rude creature. I hope he's not a sample of your Washington Territory men."

Harry grunted. "Unfortunately, he represents a certain segment, but don't judge the rest of us by that boor. There are all kinds of men here and most treat folks the way they deserve to be treated."

"Meaning what?" Alice wanted to know.

"Meaning ladies are treated like ladies and the other kind—" He shrugged.

Heather felt color creep up from the modest collar of her simple summer gown the shade of spring leaves. She had seen a few of those "other kind" during her brief Seattle stay.

"When are we going to be married?" Alice demanded. Her flaxen curls bounced and her blue eyes sparkled. One lace-mitted hand lay tucked into the crook of her fiance's elbow; on his other side, Heather's hand performed a similar act.

His face flushed with rich color when he looked down at her. "That's what I wanted to ask you. Our regular minister got called back East to a sick mother a while back. I've been filling in for him by speaking on Sundays in our little church. Not really preaching," he modestly added. "More like reading Scripture and commenting the way Mother used to do with us." His quick glance at Heather brought a flood of memories.

"But you can't marry yourself!" Alice protested. "Why don't we just get married now? There must be at least one more preacher here."

"Of course." Harry's forehead knotted. "It's just that I—we, uh, Alice, I can't get married without Blarney. He's the brother I never had."

"I suppose it would be all right for me to live at your house since Heather's there," Alice said doubtfully. "Except she's single and I don't know if Mama would consider me properly chaperoned." She gazed trustfully into Harry's face and his twin knew as far as Alice was concerned, he could fix anything on earth. Not a bad way for a bride to feel, she thought.

"Why don't you simply ask a preacher to ride out to the little church as soon as possible?" she suggested. "The few days in between won't matter." A bright idea struck her. "Harry, didn't you say your friend's cabin is finished? You can stay with him until after the wedding, can't you?"

"The Blarney Castle! The very thing. Why didn't I think of it?" He beamed and it reflected in the feminine version of his happy face. "We'll go see about it now."

Before they arrived they came upon a little group of men who knew Harry. "Hey, Templeton, is this your young lady?" Although the speaker and his cronies wore rough clothing, they respectfully removed hats and caps. "And this has to be your sister."

Harry introduced them and explained his errand. The men guffawed and said, "You shoulda been here earlier. Some excitement. A young man found the Mercer girl he wanted but when the parson asked her age, it turned out she was only seventeen."

"What happened?" Alice's blue eyes looked rounder than ever and she moved closer to Harry.

"Well, the parson up and told her Territorial rules said a gal had to be over 18 to get hitched. Felt sorry for her and the boy, too, standing there waiting." A wide grin creased his face and the others laughed, obviously knowing what happened. "I'll be a clam if the parson doesn't up and write *18* on a couple hunks of paper, stuff them in the bride's shoes and perform the ceremony, all legal-like 'cause she was *over 18*!"

Heather gasped. What kind of country had she come to, where kindness bred trickery? Yet she couldn't help feeling glad for the girl-bride.

It didn't take long to make arrangements; a minister agreed to come the following Sunday afternoon. Harry rejoiced. Now his logger and church friends could be there, along with Brian. "I'll have Blarney stand up with me, " he planned while the carriage jounced along the next morning in the clear air. "Alice, you'll want Heather, of course." If he saw how the girls clung to the sides of the buggy seat to keep from being jolted clean out of it, he gave no sign. "There's wild roses in bloom and the women'll outdo themselves decorating and hey, the camp cook, can makes us a wedding cake!"

"You mean you just walk up to him and tell him we need a cake?" Alice looked astonished but pleased.

"Sure. He's got a lighter hand with cakes and pies and stuff than any fancy New York baker," Harry bragged.

Heather smiled and concentrated on the magnificent scenery around her. Only the rolling carriage wheels and creaking of the buggy plus an occasional snort by one of the team broke silence punctuated by birdcalls. Puget Sound shone sapphire beneath a matching sky. A hundred shades of green turned the forest into a wonderland. Even the uncomfortable ride couldn't dim her joy.

Alice turned to her, face aglow with love and happiness. "Aren't you glad we came?"

"With all my heart," Heather fervently replied.

"What's that?" Harry asked when they stopped for lunch and his sister carefully lifted her long skirts to avoid knocking over her precious but prickly plant. "Not—it's heather!" The look in his eyes made the nuisance of sheltering it all the thousands of miles worthwhile. "We'll have a bit of the old home."

"Will it grow here?"

"No reason it shouldn't. If you could keep it alive on the ship, it will survive anything. Besides, it's sturdy, just what's needed to take root and grow in this new territory."

Heather tucked the plant back out of the way and his words in her heart, to be taken out and examined later.

When they came to the fork in the road and turned, Harry stammered, "Remember, this is a poor man's cabin, not a fine mansion." He laughed nervously.

Heather and Alice exchanged glances. How many times had they discussed this moment and agreed, no matter how crude or unattractive Harry's abode might be, neither must show by look or word an ounce of disappointment. Now Alice surreptitiously squeezed her friend's arm in silent reminder. "This road is like riding through a cool green tunnel," she cried in a high-pitched voice. "The interlaced branches make a canopy and with the sun shining through, why, it's beautiful!"

With the insight of twinship, Heather could feel Harry visibly relax. "Wait until you see the clearing," he promised. "The cabin's not much but the view of Mount Rainier is spectacular." His strong hands guided the team out of the green tunnel's mouth and into a cleared area, as unexpected in the sea of trees as a diamond in a mud puddle. The horses sped up a bit and the buggy rolled past a garden fenced with peeled poles and coarse wire, through abundant emerald grass. Straight ahead Harry's cabin roosted on the ground like a brood hen, lovingly protected by trees so tall they appeared to be stretching to reach the base of snowcapped Mount Rainier in the background. Heather found it hard to believe the mountain actually stood miles away, it looked so close.

For once, Alice remained silent, staring at the peak with an expression that matched Heather's feelings. Not until Harry called, "Halloo, Blarney," did either of the girls lower their gaze to their new home. Alice spoke first. "Harry Templeton, you didn't prepare us for this." She sounded choky and Heather sent a silent prayer upwards for strength—and for her twin. Alice's working face showed utter shock.

"I tried." He sounded defeated. "I know the cabin isn't much, but someday we can—"

"Isn't much!" His fiancee's blue eyes blazed. "Why, it's the coziest, friendliest, most welcoming place I've ever seen, and he, you, had us—me, at least, thinking I'd be living in a shack!"

Disillusionment changed to ecstasy. "You like it?"

"I love it," Alice cried. "Even if there had been nothing but a tent, having that mountain for a neighbor would be enough." Happy tears poured. "Oh, Harry, I'd live anywhere as long as I could be with you, but why didn't you tell us what a wonderful home you'd prepared?"

He didn't speak until they pulled up in front of the wide porch. "I guess I saw it through Eastern eyes and compared it with your home there," he quietly said.

"Foolish boy, don't you know my home is where you are?"

Heather bent and picked up her precious plant to give them a bit of privacy. She heard Harry leap from the buggy and felt it lurch when he lifted laughing Alice down. She took a deep breath, straightened and looked into the bluest eyes she had ever seen, eyes wearing an expression she could not identify but that quickened her heartbeat.

"Welcome to Washington Territory, Miss Templeton. May I be for taking that?" His rich voice and out-stretched hand freed her from her daze.

"Why, yes." She held out the little bush. A few bruised purple-rose blossoms still clung to it.

"Faith, 'tis heather you have." Brian stared at it almost reverently, deep feeling plain in his eyes. "We must plant it, soon. When it grows large enough, colleen, would you give me a cutting for near my cabin door to remind of the land I left so long ago?"

"I'll be happy to do so." She smiled and Harry, with a whoop, tore himself free from Alice's excitement and helped his sister from the buggy.

"Blarney, the outside of the cabin passed muster. It did, didn't it, Heather? Alice loves it but you haven't said."

"I love it." Her quick response left no doubt.

"Now for the inside."

"If it looks as good as it smells, you're a genius," she told him. "Oh, but it's good to be with you again." She swallowed hard. Harry's quick hug showed he understood, just as he always had.

"Heather, come in here quick," Alice called from the cabin.

"Hey, woman, you were supposed to wait for me to carry you across the threshold," her sweetheart protested. He ignored the steps, cleared the porch in a leap and disappeared through the open door.

"Miss Templeton?" Brian stepped aside to let her enter.

"You must be Mr. O'Rourke, although my brother has forgotten his manners. Not that I blame him," she hastily added, lest he think her too critical.

"Just Brian, although the loggers have another name for me." His ever-changing blue gaze held little gold twinkles.

"Very well, Mr. Brian. I suppose, since we'll be neighbors, there's no need for Eastern formality. Please call me Heather."

"It's for being a lovely name."

For a moment the weeks and months vanished. Again she stood in Adelaide's room watching her preening stepmother. Again she heard the unkind words, *The only pretty thing about you is your ridiculous name . . .only a heathen would name her child after a bush.* She averted her face so the red-haired Irishman wouldn't see how the memory had blighted her arrival. "Is that roast beef I smell?" She stepped inside. A quick glance took in whitewashed walls, spotlessness, a laid table, a bearskin rug and stopped short. "Apple pies? Harry, you never baked those! Mr. Brian, are you a magician as well as a sailor and logger and gardener and homebuilder?" She felt the gaiety that had been suppressed for years breaking its bonds.

"It's a venison roast, but the pies came from the logging camp cook shack."

Alice spun in a mad whirl and ended up looking into Brian's smiling face. "He's going to make our wedding cake, the camp cook, I mean, and Harry has to stay with you at the Blarney Castle because we won't get married until Sunday afternoon and Heather's single and can't be my chaperone and the preacher's coming and you're going to be best man and. . ." She ran out of breath.

Heather liked the way Brian's eyes twinkled while he solemnly said, "This is for being exciting, but perhaps we should eat while the food is tasty and talk later. If you ladies wish to freshen yourselves—not that you look as if you need it—there's a basin and water and soap and towels in the bedrooms."

"Alice, our room is the one on the right." Harry pointed. "Heather, you'll be on the left."

A delicate blush came to the bride-to-be's face at the words *our room* and a soft light to her eyes. A dozen times during the meal that followed the new arrivals' quick washing up, the same look returned. Heather saw love, trust and a deep, abiding happiness; they silently shouted her friend's joy. After the delicious meal that left her feeling she could never eat again, she considerately shooed Harry and Alice out. "I'll wash up," she said firmly. The fact neither protested made her lips twitch.

"I'll help," Brian offered. He added a bit diffidently, "If Miss Heather wants a bit of a walk, I'll show her the O'Rourke Palace."

"You mean the Blarney Castle," Harry corrected and Alice's trill of laughter when they hurried out showed her appreciation of the nickname.

"It's much smaller than this," Brian explained. "In one way, I'm for liking it better."

"Why is that?" Heather's capable hands stilled in

the dishwater, poured into pans from a steaming kettle and tempered with icy water from the bucket Brian said he'd carried earlier in the afternoon. He had also explained one of the first things he and Harry had done after they came was clean out the well on the place so the water would be pure and drinkable.

"I think I'll let you see for yourself. Come. If we don't go now, you won't be able to get the effect I want you to have."

None of the young men of her acquaintance had intrigued Heather as did this cheerful stranger who didn't seem strange at all. She confidently followed him in the worn path across the clearing, through an uncut stand of trees he said would never be logged except for those that must come out to give room for others to grow and into another clearing, smaller than in front of her brother's place. A second cabin clung to the ground but when they reached it, Brian said, "Turn your back on the hut and see my living tapestry."

Heather obeyed—and stood speechless. Twilight behind Mount Rainier had turned its snow to lavender frosting with purple highlights. Bright stars had already begun to glow. A lopsided moon inspected the world and smiled at the humans who had invaded its domain. Heather remained transfixed until Brian again said, "Come."

She looked at him in the moonlight, just a few inches taller than her 5'7" height but strong and sturdy as the mountain above them. "If you don't mind, may we see your home another time?" She couldn't explain her unwillingness to destroy the sight they had just witnessed by entering a cabin, no matter how comfortable it might be.

"Such nights make a man feel the Creator is for being near," he said quietly and led the way back. His stride never faltered even when the only light came from the moon and starshine sifting through the branches in the wooded area.

"Can you see in the dark?" she whispered.

"Don't be afraid, Miss Heather. I've trod this trail many times before when 'twas much blacker than this."

"I'm not afraid." Heather couldn't have told why. Something in the square-shouldered figure marching ahead of her with head up as if he carried banners offered mute reassurance.

Across the larger clearing they walked, in light silver-soft as the veil of a princess. Used to swains who attempted liberties or grew sentimental with every moment alone, Heather appreciated Brian O'Rourke's silence. He never touched her until they reached Harry's cabin and only then to lay a restraining hand on her arm and whisper, "Shhh. Turn slowly to your left."

She followed orders. Her hand flew to her mouth to stifle a cry. Halfway between where they stood and the forest that encroached on the clearing, a doe and two fawns daintily stepped forward. The bright night clearly showed large, pale spots on the fawns. In fascinated wonder, Heather watched them come, unafraid, splendid.

Brian gave a sharp whistle. The doe's head snapped up. He whistled again and away she went, her fawns bounding after her, white tails in the air like tiny flags. "We don't want them too friendly," Brian explained. "They're so curious and eager to get into the garden, we've had to fortify the fence or not have fresh vegetables."

Heather didn't once connect the animals she had seen with the excellent roast served at supper!

A little later, Harry and Brian departed for the Blarney Castle, leaving the newcomers in sole possession of the cabin. "Will you be afraid to stay alone?" Harry had worried aloud.

"Should we be?" Alice demanded.

"No. We can be here in minutes, if needed."

His fiancee placed her hands on her hips and said with a hint of exasperation in her voice, "Harry Templeton, tell me how you'll know we need you if we wake in the middle of the night and you're sound asleep in the Blarney Castle clear over there in the northwest corner."

"Hmmm." He considered, then bolted out the door. "I know."

"What's he up to?" Alice asked but Brian just shook his head until a melodious clanging sounded, then he laughed.

Harry charged back in triumphantly bearing a cowbell and ringing it for all its worth. "Compliments of the former tenant," he said.

"Stop it," Heather told him between giggles. "You'll wake the neighbors." She giggled again. "And the bears and deer and whatever else is out in those woods."

He desisted and his laughter fled. "One thing, you're going to have to learn to shoot. Until you do, stay close to the house. There are wild animals in the woods; they usually stay there, but not always. Never get so far from the house you can't get back unless you have a gun with you. And never, under any circumstances, try to outrun a bear. Even a good horse can't always do that. Climb a tree, if possible, but pick the right one. You have to get higher than a bear will follow and be in a tree sturdy enough so you can't be shaken out of its branches."

"What else do we need to know?" Alice shivered.

"Don't get near a cub. They're cute and tempting but more than one person has been clawed by mama for coming too close to her cubs."

"What about mountain lions?" Heather asked from her limited store of knowledge gained by tales heard on the *Scotland*.

"We call them cougars," Harry explained. "With the logging camp so close, there's not a lot of danger. Again, if you ever find some cuddly oversized kittens, leave them be and hightail it for home. Normally, cougars are cowardly. Unless provoked or driven out of the mountains because of early snow and no available food, they don't jump adults."

"You mean they've attacked children?"

"There are stories among the Indians," Harry mumbled.

Brian quickly added, "That was far from here and shows a lot of resourcefulness. An Indian girl and her little brother were said to be away from camp late one fall when early snows in the mountains had driven the deer to lower elevations. A scrawny, hungry beast came and went for the boy. The girl snatched up a stout tree limb and drove the cougar away before he could do more than scratch up the child."

Alice fearfully looked around. "I'm glad there are

windows. Cougars and bears don't jump through windows, do they?"

"No, and by winter we'll have heavy shutters," Harry comforted. "Besides, I'm a good shot and can protect my family."

Yet in spite of his soothing, after the men left Alice pulled the bright curtains shut, and insisted they both sleep in the larger bed in her room, although Heather would rather have been alone to sort out all the things that had happened since she reached the clearing, and watch the moonlit night from uncurtained windows.

nine

Tired from the trip and the excitement of finally reaching their journey's end, the travelers slept long and deeply. Heather awakened to silence that sharply contrasted with the usual ship noises. For a moment she couldn't figure out where she was, except that the bed on which she lay felt far softer than her accustomed resting place these past months. She sniffed. Why did it smell like the outdoors?

With an effort, she turned her head, saw Alice's flaxen hair in the two long braids she wove at night and sat up straight, eyes wide. How could they sleep on this first morning in their new home? She started to nudge her friend and thought better of it. Instead, she slipped from bed, straightened her rumpled nightgown and padded barefoot to the window, smiling at the closed curtains. A quick push sent them aside and revealed a glorious day.

"Why has the ship stopped?" A sleepy demand sent her back to tower over the bed. Alice opened her eyes and yawned. Recognition chased away sleep's shadows. "Oh, we're here."

"Yes, and isn't it wonderful?"

"It will be when I wake up." She raised her head and a sunbeam shone full in her face. "The curtains! Quick, Heather, run into the other rooms and open the curtains. Harry will never let me hear the last of it if he finds out. Where is he, anyway? What time is it?"

"My dear innocent, Harry and Mr. O'Rourke have jobs. They've probably been gone for hours. I don't know much about woodswork, but I suspect they don't wait until nearly noon to begin their day."

Alice looked remorseful. "Poor dears, they didn't have any breakfast or we would have heard them."

"I'm not so sure about that." Heather laughed and slid into a lightweight wrapper. "The way I slept, six bears and ten cougars, complete with cubs, could have come to call and I wouldn't have heard a thing. I imagine the men went early and had breakfast in the cook shack. Speaking of breakfast, I'm starved."

"You can't be after all the dinner you ate last night." Alice reached for her robe.

"That's what you think. Come on, let's see what we can find."

A quick survey of the kitchen showed bread, eggs, a ham, marmalade ready to be used and a pot of coffee still faintly warm.

"Mercy, they've been here." Alice's face reflected dismay. "They must have seen the curtains."

"Who cares?" Heather flung the door wide and let the warm day flow in. "They won't expect us to be perfect, at least until we've been here a week or two. Now, Miss Freeman, set the table while I fry ham and eggs, and toast some of that bread."

"In less than a week, I'll be getting up and making breakfast for Harry," Alice said.

"I've been wondering about that. Just because I'm living with you, I don't want to play gooseberry all the time. How would you like for me to stay in bed and let you have breakfast alone with your new husband?"

Alice turned pink. "I—would you mind, I mean, just at first?"

"Not at all." Heather shook her head, although a little envy at the thought of the intimate breakfasts cropped up. "I'll get to sleep longer. Besides, if Harry leaves practically at dawn, won't you want to go back to bed for a time?"

"Yes. Except, what about Brian?"

"I'm sure he doesn't expect to eat with us all the time, especially breakfast," Heather observed. "He seems very sensitive to others' feelings. Once I mention what I plan to do, he will catch on, I'm sure. He's a good cook so he won't starve."

"Oh, but we'll want him here for meals, for supper, at least," Alice protested. "Why, if he hadn't helped Harry we'd not have this fine cabin." She looked anxiously around the tasteful home in the wilderness.

"The sensible thing is to ask Harry." Heather cut off a piece of bread. "This is unusual, isn't it? I wonder if the camp cook made it?"

"Maybe." But Alice's conversation skipped from subject to subject like a log roller on a mill pond. "Will you wear your green dress when you stand up with me? It makes your eyes look green."

"With jealousy. You'll be the prettiest bride ever to be married in Washington Territory. If I ever marry, people will say, 'how nice she looks, but isn't her matron of honor lovely'?"

"Don't say such things even in jest," Alice pleaded. "You're better than pretty."

"What do you mean?"

"Everywhere you go you see blond-haired, blue-eyed, so-called pretty girls like me. You don't see tall young women with a cloud of soft brown hair and the most beautiful hazel eyes in the whole world."

The sincerity in her voice brought a rich blush to Heather's smooth cheeks. Alice ran for a looking glass that had come with her from the East. "See? When your eyes sparkle with laughter and you blush, you're absolutely lovely."

To Heather's amazement, the face in the glass little resembled the cowed Heather Templeton scorned by Adelaide. The image's tumbled hair and happy face sent pride into her heart and the secret knowledge Adelaide had been wrong about her looks, as well as so many other things. . .

Brian O'Rourke had done his work so well, it left little need for more than some straightening. Once Heather and Alice brushed the crumbs from the cloth and did their few dishes, the younger girl sat down to plan dinner after an extensive survey of the wealth of stores on hand. Heather wandered out to the shed, now empty of horses, and came back with a small shovel. She lured Alice from her study of recipes long enough to help decide where they should plant the heather, then lingered over her task and lovingly patted the bush when she finished. "Someday there will be a great patch here by the steps," she murmured. "As soon as it gets large enough to be separated, a cutting must go to the O'Rourke Palace."

Blissfully unaware she had designated the second cabin by Brian's name choice rather than the more undignified Blarney Castle, Heather put away her shovel, watered the plant, and went to wash her hands, thinking of the redheaded man who appeared so gentle, but who—according to Harry—could lick his weight in cougars.

She continued to wonder in the days that followed. Each night the sound of hoofbeats and a, "Hi-o, the cabin," heralded the men's return from their jobs. Brian and Harry always waved when the girls hurried to the doorway, then rode on to the Blarney Castle to clean up and shave before coming to the bountiful suppers guaranteed to fill and satisfy even their huge appetites. On nice evenings, Heather drove her twin and Alice outdoors for a stroll, secretly rejoicing when Brian matter-of-factly helped her with the dishes and clearing up. In those moments, she learned of his boyhood and long years at sea. She saw far more than what his words implied and sensed the deep loneliness that had been temporarily assuaged by Captain Haines' friendship, then vanquished when he came to Seattle and met Harry. In turn, Heather found herself sharing feelings formerly hidden or at best, merely hinted at with Alice.

"Before Harry went away I always had someone," she said. "I hope it doesn't sound selfish, but after he'd gone, I had to accept I was no longer first with anyone in the whole world."

"Not even the lads I'm sure came calling?" Brian's gentle smile robbed his question of impertinence.

"Oh, them. What few passed Adelaide and Father's rigid inspection—which meant they had to be rich and of an elite family—bored me until I felt I'd scream." She laughed and it rang in the quiet cabin. "Not a one of them could do the work you and Harry do or build a cabin. Most of them wouldn't even know how to ride a horse."

"It takes sturdy folk to tame this land and it will be tamed," Brian predicted. He finished drying the last sparkling dish and hung the dish towel on a nail to dry. "Shall we be for joining the others? It's such a nice evening, I'm thinking it's time for a lesson in shooting."

"Really?" Heather's breath quickened. "I'm excited and a little fearful, as well. Must we learn?"

The curly red head nodded emphatically and the blue eyes turned serious. "Indeed. God be thanked if you never need to use the skill but you and Miss Alice have to be prepared. This is a wild country."

When Heather looked down the rifle barrel for the first time, it appeared to be a mile long. She gripped it tightly, pressing the end of Harry's rifle that he called the butt firmly against her shoulder and her hands where he directed. She obediently sighted but her first shot whistled harmlessly past the rude target he'd drawn and nailed to a stump. Her second shot also went wild but her third shot actually nicked the edge of the heavy paper.

"Good. Now you, Alice," Harry encouraged.

Heather wanted to laugh at the sight of Alice looking along the rifle barrel. The tip of her pink tongue showed between her teeth and determination flashed in her round eyes. She did a little better; her second shot hit the target and so did her third. The girls took turnabout practice until the patient sun tired of watching and went to bed for the night.

"Well, that's that." Heather gave a little skip on the

way back to the cabin.

"Not so fast, young lady." Harry fixed a stern gaze on her. "You have to know how to load and clean a weapon before you get out of my firing school." He proceeded to teach his small class and drilled them until both could properly load, unload, and clean.

Alice said with mock innocence, "And here we thought all we had to do out here was to take care of you, Harry." It brought a laugh and ended the lesson.

"Now that you know which end the bullets go in, you can practice tomorrow," Harry loftily told them but his pride in sweetheart and sister gleamed in his hazel eyes.

The following Sunday afternoon a tremulous Alice, gowned in white and momentarily subdued by the fulfillment of her years of dreams, took Harry Templeton's firm hand and became his wife in a simple but touching ceremony. The little log church bloomed lovely as the bride, decked in wild roses and a few precious flowers from the pioneer wives' carefully tended gardens. Harry wore the tiniest of heather sprigs from the plant outside his door. If the surroundings didn't match the stately church back East where Alice would have been married, the friendliness of loggers and settlers made up for it. The few women had begged to make it a time of feasting and Heather saw how well they did with limited resources. The camp cook's wedding cake glistened in four layers and topped off the meal, a poem in white frosting.

The wife of a straw boss sidled up to Heather when the festivities drew to a close. Kindness radiated from her plain face. "Child, my man and I'd be happy to

have you stay a spell with us; a day or two so the young-
uns can have a bit of a honeymoon."

"Why, thank you." Heather looked around for Harry.
She caught his glance and motioned him over. The good
woman repeated her invitation.

The groom smiled and a tender look crept into his
face. "We thank you, but the honeymoon has to come
later. I'll be going to work tomorrow morning as usual
and I'd rather have my sister there with Alice."

"For certain," the hospitable woman hastily said. "I
didn't know your plans."

"We want to save our money and maybe later I can
take time off when the snow's out of the mountains.
Alice wants to go camping and it's still too early."

Brian O'Rourke, resplendent in his dark suit and role
of best man, spoke from behind Heather. His smile
blazed beneath the wet-down red curls. "I see it's time
for me to be springing my surprise. Miss Heather, I'll
be honored if you'll stay at the O'Rourke Palace for a
day or two. I have business in Seattle. You'd still be
with your new sister during the day and could take the
cowbell with you."

His remark called forth an explanation of the girls'
system of summoning help if needed and a wave of
laughter followed.

"What's all this business in Seattle you suddenly need
to do?" Harry asked suspiciously.

"Why, I didn't say, did I?" He appeared to withdraw
to within himself. "Don't worry. I haven't gone and
got myself fired, if that's what you're thinking." Despite the others' curiosity, he refused to say more.

That night Heather lay alone in the smaller cabin,

the first time since she left the East Coast. The cowbell sat on the floor beside her. Not that she expected to need it. The few rustlings in the night she and Alice had heard since they arrived turned out to be a chuckling porcupine on a moonlight stroll. It had left the girls giggling when they bravely peered out the window before ringing an alarm. A strange feeling pervaded her, not fear or even loneliness, more a melancholy that had to do with the realization her father might never know Harry had taken on the responsibilities of a husband unless the Freemans told him. Although she had written news of their arrival and sent it off before coming to the cabin in the buggy, she knew Adelaide's temperament included ruthlessly destroying any communication from her stepchildren, then using their lack of contact as another wedge to further embitter Harrison. The cast-off daughter fell asleep against a wet pillow, a prayer in her heart that one day the estrangement would end.

Alice bounced in bright and early the next morning. A sunbonnet partially covered her hair and she carried Harry's rifle. "Mrs. Templeton calling on Miss Templeton," she caroled. Then in her usual practical way she abandoned her pose and said, "Having you stay over here is silly. Come home where you belong." She slipped an arm through Heather's. "Harry and I agreed before he left for work the house doesn't seem right without our sister there. Don't bother to argue. It won't do you any good."

She shepherded her charge through picking up the few items she had brought to Brian's cabin and back through the trees across the meadow, and bent double laughing when Heather meekly raised an eyebrow and retorted, "You're the one with the gun. Do you always take it when you go calling, Mrs. Templeton?"

"Harry says we're to keep it nearby," Alice smugly reminded. "Harry says it's better to be ready than sorry. Harry says the way life works, if we have the rifle we'll never need it but if we don't have it, we will, if you understand what I mean."

"I understand you're in danger of becoming one of those wives who never has an idea of her own but quotes her man as though he knew everything in the world," Heather told her.

"You mean he doesn't?" Alice couldn't hold back laughter. "You know better than that, but Harry *does* know a whole lot more about Washington Territory than we do and if we're smart, we'll listen and learn." She broke off. "I'm dying of curiosity to find out why Brian took off like that. Harry has no idea, either."

"So there *is* something my brother doesn't know," Heather teased and ran ahead of Alice to escape her quick chase, little realizing the predicament that had sent their Irish friend post-haste to the city.

৯

Miles away, Brian walked the streets of Seattle, heart heavy and filled with defeat. He had been unable to discover the information desperately needed. What could he do now? No one seemed to know what he sought or if they did, they guarded it closely. How could he go back and tell. . . At this point, his fine lips set in a straight line. His face set like a granite ledge, immovable. The hardest thing he'd ever been forced to do had been to keep up a cheerful pretense and not spoil his friends' wedding. If Harry had known what came up late on Saturday night, of the secret visit to the Blarney Castle, the whispered confrontation, the most wonderful day of young Templeton's life would have forever carried the taint betrayal leaves on innocent persons involved only because of friendship.

Just to be sure no further knowledge could be gained by staying, Brian silently whispered a prayer for wisdom but the doors to the news he needed remained bolted against him. Late Tuesday afternoon he began his long ride back. He'd only been given two days off and the straw boss had looked suspicious when Brian insisted this was an emergency but refused to disclose the nature of his need to be gone.

What a different homecoming from all the times he and Harry rode gaily home, physically tired from their hard day's work but with anticipation of the evening to follow! Brian realized how in the few days Heather and Alice had been there, they had provided the missing element to make the cabin home complete. He thought of Harry's twin, a welcoming smile when she saw them, her beautiful eyes glowing over a panful of dirty dishes, the walks and talks that had taken them so far on the road toward friendship. He thought of how she would react once she learned the reason for his journey to Seattle. "God, why is life so hard?" he cried. His only answer came with the stilling of bird song, the turn of his horse's head and quick snort.

He reached the turnoff, the clearing. Dusk lay heavy; a light in the cabin window showed his chance of detection slight. He swerved so Harry's horse in the shed wouldn't sense his own mount's presence and nicker, then rode to the stand of timber that lay between clearings. No yellow light escaped from the O'Rourke Palace. Either Heather had gone to bed early or the newlyweds had taken her to their cabin. Good. He went on past, glad his horse had traveled this way many times. Dread in his heart, mouth dry, Brian gritted his teeth, let his horse pick the way, and wondered if the crazy, upside-down world he'd plunged into after last Saturday night could ever be turned around and set straight again. At the present moment, the likelihood of that happening loomed smaller than minnows in a secluded forest pond.

Hours later he returned, bone-weary and conscious of how little time lay between now and rising time. Yet he paced the floor, brow wrinkled. Could he have done more? He shook his head. At least for now, nothing remained to be done except to wait—and that offered no solution. Time itself allowed for no more waiting.

At last Brian flung himself on his bed for a bare two hours sleep. He awakened to a grand morning and memories of the past few days hit him like a twisting tree. Before long, the man he loved and called brother, the young woman he had admitted in the dark night hours he one day hoped to call wife, the sneering, finger-pointing world would know the truth. But far from making free, as the Scriptures said, that same truth already winged like a terrible, avenging angel, destroying lives.

At the end of day, he thanked God for Harry's abstraction and his focus on Alice that kept him from seeing the disturbance Brian felt he miserably failed to hide. Pleading the need to make up for sleep lost on his errand, he sidetracked eating supper at the big cabin and headed for his own place. His quick glimpse of Heather in Harry's doorway, hand upraised and wearing a large white apron, had set his heart to pounding. If only he could be with her! He rejected the idea immediately. He must have time to think, to clear his muddled mind before he again stood in her presence. So he waved, managed to call a greeting and rode on as if all were well, with the instinctive seeking of solitude known to every wounded animal of the forest. Yet unlike the fox or wolf or coyote that finds in its lair a place to heal, the Blarney Castle felt more like prison than a refuge. The laws of God and man had been broken. Now, the full price must be paid—and soon.

ten

Heather, the woman, and heather, the transplanted shrub, took root in the rich Washington Territory soil and thrived. Except for the continuing silence in response to her letters, she found herself happier than since her mother died. Just being with her twin brought joy and Alice truly loved her in a sisterly way. As for Brian O'Rourke. . . Heather always broke off her thoughts at this point although she knew warmth and color came to her neck and face above the modest collar of her simple cotton gowns. In an effort to be unobtrusive in the first weeks and months of her brother's marriage, she naturally turned to the Irishman, basking in the growing admiration she saw in his Puget Sound blue eyes.

A certain mid-summer evening set the admiration blazing into something more intense. Brian and Heather had lingered alongside the shining stream he loved to fish, little heeding the passing of time. Loath to end their time together, the young woman treasured every sight and sound of forest and sky, packing away each changing expression on her companion's face to remember later, the way housewives put meat and vegetables away in brine to be taken out when needed. How dear he had become, this man with the honest face and open expression. The magic of territorial summer had woven gossamer webs and brought them to a friendship Heather had not known before. Friendship? She felt her lips curve in a smile and her heart beat faster. Nay, more than that.

"We'd better be for heading home." Brian sighed and rose from the stream bank. "Dark will catch us if we're not careful."

"I won't be afraid."

A poignant look crept into his eyes. "I hope, colleen, you'll never be afraid when you're with me." Heaviness replaced his former gladness and she sensed his reluctance to break the spell of the place and moment, but walked behind him after he collected the string of fish and shouldered the rifle he always carried on their jaunts.

They had almost reached the clearing around the Blarney Castle when a slight rustle in the bushes along the path froze Heather and dried her throat to a crisp. "What's that?"

"Wait." He took a few steps forward and slid the rifle off his shoulder. Less than a heartbeat later, something exploded from the bushes, a long, tawny something that snarled and pounced.

Hampered by the string of fish, Brian nevertheless swung his rifle toward the attacker but too late. The frenzied cougar hit man and gun full force, sending Brian to the ground and the rifle flying.

"Run," he screamed, from the spitting cat's embrace.

Heather saw him desperately clutching the beast's throat before they rolled over and over in the trail. Run? When the man she loved lay fighting a menace like this? Anger and strength welled up within her and she raced forward, shouting at the top of her lungs. Surely

Harry would hear and come—but would he arrive too late? Even the growing dusk couldn't conceal the blood on Brian's set face from the initial impact of the crouched cat.

"God, help us!" she cried, her gaze wildly searching for a downed limb, anything to beat off the cougar. From the corner of her eye she saw the rifle lying a few yards away. "God, please, don't let it be broken," she pleaded.

Gathering her skirt folds out of the way, she leaped past the fighting duet, snatched the rifle, and turned. Brian and the cougar rolled again. Like one in a trance she lifted her weapon, remembered the instructions and practice she'd received, and aimed. Despair ran through her. How could she keep from hitting Brian? Cold sweat popped out on her forehead. She pressed the butt of the rifle more firmly to her shoulder and sighted. She must hit the furious cat without shooting Brian and now, before the Irishman weakened. "God, hear my prayer," she whispered. Eyes wide open, hands steady, she waited until the tawny head appeared in her sights and pulled the trigger.

The bullet apparently grazed the cougar for it snarled, loosened its hold and turned from its prey. Trembling inside but rock-firm on the outside, Heather shot again. This time the cougar leaped into the air. She sent another bullet toward it—and missed completely. The great cat crouched for its spring toward the new and deadlier enemy. Something inside her told Heather to wait. Her fourth shot caught the cat in mid-leap. Without wavering, she put her last two bullets into the foe that collapsed to the forest floor inches from her feet.

It lay still but she didn't trust her own marksmanship so she grabbed the rifle by the barrel, dimly aware of its length and unwieldiness. If the cougar moved she'd use the heavy stock as a club.

Not until Brian struggled to a standing position and staggered to her saying, "It's dead, thanks be to you and our Father," did she release her death grip on the rifle and realize how the palms of her hands shook from the strain they'd been under.

"Heather, *mavourneen*."* Strong arms caught her close.

She sagged, yet the feeling she had come home ran through her like a crown fire sweeps through dry timber. For a moment, she stood supported by his strong arms, then in the last rays of daylight she looked into his bloodstained face and jerked free of his encircling arms. "Lie down," she ordered. "You're badly hurt."

Comprehension born of returning understanding now that the danger had passed came into his eyes. "Why, I am." He reached for his head and she saw claw marks on his arms through the rents in his shirt sleeves. He stumbled a bit and she eased him to the ground, then without embarrassment yanked off a petticoat, tore great strips, and made a pad for the bleeding head wounds. "Can you hold it on?"

"Sure." His fingers tightened on the makeshift bandage.

Heather ripped what was left of the shirtsleeves away, exposing deep scratches on flesh white as her own from shoulder to sun-bronzed wrist. Dusk prevented her from a full examination but they didn't appear as deep or serious as the scratches on Brian's face. She hastily
*my darling

wound the remainder of her petticoat around his arms, ordered him to stay put, and set off for Harry and Alice's cabin at a dead run. Several times her feet slipped on the grassy path in the Blarney Castle clearing. The stretch of woods that separated it from the one in front of her brother's cabin loomed dark and unfriendly. What a difference it made when Brian accompanied her.

Out of breath and nearly spent, she stumbled and fell but picked herself up and continued. What felt like a lifetime later, Heather bolted out of the woods—and head-on into a solid mass.

"God, help me," she screamed, then collapsed against Harry's chest.

"It's all right, Heather, I heard shots and—"

"Brian," she sobbed. "A cougar."

The sound of running steps heralded Alice's arrival. She carried a lighted lantern that relentlessly showed Heather's bloodstained hands and dress. "*Dear God, what is it?*"

"I'm all right." Heather pushed her twin away. "Brian's hurt. I'll show you."

"You go back to the cabin with Alice," Harry ordered. "I'll take care of Brian. I'll need the lantern, though. Alice, can you get her there?"

"Of course." She took Heather's arm. "Come on. Harry will take care of everything." The lantern bobbed, then disappeared. Alice wisely asked no questions until they reached the cabin. Never had anything on earth looked so good to Heather as the open door with yellow lamplight streaming out. Alice cared for her like a little child and refused to let her speak until settled into a handmade chair by the fireplace.

"Now, what happened?"

Sheer horror tightened her friend's throat and it took all the grit she possessed to recall the near-tragedy in the forest. Again she heard the bushes rustle. Again she saw that leaping creature and felt her own helplessness in the first moments of the attack. She finished with, "I don't know how badly he's hurt. A lot of blood came."

"It always does from a head wound," Alice reminded.

Heather struggled from the chair, aware her knees had turned to jelly. "We should have gone back with Harry," she wildly cried. "Oh, Alice, if Brian dies, what will I do?" Pretense about her newly-discovered feelings fled before the stern reality she might lose Brian without him ever knowing she cared.

"He's not going to die," Alice stoutly told her, pale-faced but determined. "Where's your faith, Heather Templeton?" Yet even she quailed a bit when Harry came in with Brian draped across his shoulders.

"He looks worse than he's hurt," Harry quickly reassured, before lowering their friend into a chair. "Soon as we get the blood off him you'll see." He deftly unwound the bandages Heather had formed. "Good girl." A wide smile of approval stretched his face and firelight twinkled in his hazel eyes. "First she shoots a cougar, then plays nurse and does as pretty a job as you could ask for. Too bad I have to remove your fancy work but we need to see how deep the wounds are."

"I couldn't tell; it was so nearly dark," Heather said. She bit her lips to steady them and held her breath when Harry raised his head after thoroughly washing Brian's wounds and said, "They'll heal naturally. No need for stitches. Hey, pardner, you'd better be mighty thankful this sister of mine kept a cool head. That's one of the biggest cougars I've seen around here. Wonder what made it attack?"

Brian shrugged. "Loco, maybe. They get that way once in awhile." His rambling gave Heather time to pull herself together and she smiled at the patient and laid a restraining hand on him to keep him from rising.

"I-I never thought I'd see a man wrestle a mountain lion," she said. "Just rest."

The curly red head shook disagreement. "Got to get back to my palace," he mumbled.

"In a pig's eye." Harry overrode the idea. "You're staying here tonight. I don't expect any ill effects but we just won't be for taking chances."

A faint smile rewarded him. "Sure, and I'll make an Irishman out of you yet," Brian threatened. Some color stole back into his white face and sparkle to his eyes.

"We'll make you a bed in the corner," Alice promised. "Harry, go cut boughs." She went into her bedroom and came back with sweet smelling sheets and a light blanket. An hour later the cabin in the clearing lay silent except for a slight breeze that riffled the curtains through the open windows and brought with it the scent of trees and grass.

Heather lay wide-eyed and sleepless. The feelings she'd kept down earlier demanded release and threatened to overwhelm her. Would she ever forget that horrible, frozen minute when only the mercy of God gave her strength to stir and not stand aside like a white-

faced ninny? She shuddered in a repetition of the re-
vulsion that had swept through her when Harry jok-
ingly offered to skin the cougar and hang the hide on
her wall. Dead or alive, she wanted no reminders of
the tawny cat that might well have snuffed out much
of the meaning in life. She concentrated on the love
that had lain dormant, perhaps since her twin's first
mention of his friend; the love that sprang full blown
in time of peril. Heather relived the brief period in
Brian's strong arms and the security they offered. She
fell asleep to dream of blue eyes, blue skies, and a
future filled with sunlight.

A week later, Brian returned to work bearing scars
not yet healed, but in full possession of strength and
clarity of mind. A new jauntiness sat in his expression, marred only by private thoughts that came and
went, leaving him quiet and uncommunicative. If the
others noticed, they said nothing, yet a new openness
on the Irishman's part, deeper gratitude to the God who
had been merciful, colored Brian's speech. Heather,
too, spent more time on her knees, thanking her heavenly Father for the good things in life. She also hugged
to herself the ever-growing love, grateful that Alice
stayed unusually silent and didn't attempt to discuss
the situation. Just for a time, seeing that love deepen
and unfold was enough. And if Brian saw a new gentleness and suspected its source, only his gaze betrayed
him.

Into the idyllic garden of Eden existence came a serpent to despoil. Heather and Alice were first to feel its
presence. They had formed the habit of walking to the
O'Rourke Palace or Blarney Castle—depending on

which of them identified it—once a week to add their touches to the reasonably clean abode by putting up curtains, giving the windows an extra polish and such. Mindful of how the wilderness encroached to the very edge of their own little world, they always carried Harry's rifle along with cleaning equipment. One particularly nice day, they headed down the path, went through the woods and across the clearing, chattering of inconsequential things and unsuspecting. They reached the cabin and stopped short.

The door stood open.

"Why, whoever—" Alice stared and Heather's gaze followed her glance. "Brian never leaves the door open, although it's always unlocked. Do you think he is sick or something and came home?"

"I don't know." Heather called out, "Brian?"

No answer came but a slight stirring betrayed the presence of someone or something inside.

"You don't think it's another cougar, do you?" Alice took a step backwards and her face whitened. She unslung and readied the rifle.

Heather squashed the fear that rose inside her at the suggestion. "Cougars can't open doors, can they? Don't be a goose." She stepped to the porch, crossed to the open door and peered inside. A laugh of relief came and she said, "Come on in, Alice. There's nothing to be afraid of. It's Crying Dove."

"Good. We haven't seen her for some time." Alice hurried into the cabin and almost bumped into Heather, who had stopped short. The beautiful Indian girl sat staring at them. Slow tears made glistening streaks on her curiously blanched face.

"Why, Dove, are you hurt?" Heather crossed the tidy room and knelt beside the intruder.

The weeping girl bowed her head into her hands and silently shook her head. She rocked to and fro, the picture of grief too deep for words.

"What is it, Crying Dove?" Alice timidly placed one hand on the buckskin-clad shoulder.

"O'Rourke. Where is he?"

The muffled demand sent premonitory chills through Heather. What on earth—

"He promise to help me." Crying Dove's hands fell listlessly into her lap.

"Of course he will help you," Alice said. "So will we if we know that the trouble is."

The distraught girl's face contorted.

"Where is your father, Running Wolf?" Heather asked, dreading the answer without knowing why.

"Running Wolf is no longer my father. I have brought shame to him and the tribe." Crying Dove's dull eyes made her look old.

A sickening lurch of Heather's stomach left her weak, although a little voice inside passionately declared, *no. It cannot be*.

Alice looked like one awakened from sleepwalking, half dazed. "You mean you. . ." Her voice dwindled and died.

"I am with child."

Heather tasted blood from where she'd driven her teeth into her lip. She'd known some in this raw land sought Indian girls, squaw men, Harry had called them. But Brian O'Rourke? Impossible! She thought of his honest face, the respectful way he never tried to touch her. He couldn't be guilty of such a monstrous crime, could he? Yet Crying Dove repeated, "O'Rourke. He must help. I have no place to go."

The white woman's world crashed. Fury erased trust. How had Brian dared called her darling and hold her close after the cougar lay dead? Scorching shame filled her. She felt she had been profaned. An angry sob tore into her throat and she swallowed to keep it from escaping. All the time he had walked and talked with her and spoken of God, he had been secretly carrying on a clandestine affair with Crying Dove. For the first time since she fled her father's home, Heather desperately wished herself back. What did it matter what Adelaide convinced Father to do? It could never compare with this heartbreak and pain, attacking her the way the mountain lion had crouched unseen and leaped on Brian when he least expected it.

She turned before tears could come and marched out of the cabin, leaving Alice to deal with Crying Dove. Forgetting the danger of being weaponless, she dashed through the woods that pressed in on her, crossed the big clearing, and fled to the safety of her own room. Yet now that she had the privacy to cry, not one tear came. Self-loathing at having been taken in by a hypocrite who talked of God and lived with the devil brought back composure. By the time Alice arrived, disheveled and red-faced, Heather stood in the living area of the cabin waiting. "Well?"

"I don't believe it." Alice's mouth quivered. "No matter how it looks, I don't believe Brian O'Rourke is guilty." Her face crumpled into misery. "Oh, Heather, what is Harry going to say?" She threw herself into her friend's arms.

Fresh disgust and pain steeled Heather against the last ray of hope. Harry loved Brian with a brother's love. "He won't believe it."

The deadness of her response sent Alice into a spasm of sobs. Finally, she wiped her eyes on a checked dress sleeve. "There has to be some other answer."

"What? Running Wolf wouldn't cast off his only child unless her story's true."

"That doesn't mean it's Brian," Alice said weakly.

"Who else could it be? It certainly isn't Harry and Running Wolf wouldn't let any of the loggers within a mile of Crying Dove." Desolation ruthlessly checked off all explanations except the obvious, hateful as it might be. "What did she say after I left?"

"Just that Brian said he'd help."

"So he knows about this." Heather felt lightheaded. "For how long, I wonder?" She took a deep breath. "Alice—that trip to Seattle on your wedding day. You don't suppose he was making arrangements even then." Her voice dropped to a horrified whisper.

Alice turned the color of snow. "All we can do is pray."

"For whom?" Heather lashed out, too much in turmoil to care what she said. "For Crying Dove? Brian?" She laughed wildly. "Better pray for Harry and you and—and all of us who have been betrayed. How could anyone be so vile?" Could a broken heart bleed inside, the way hers felt now? Where were the ideals Captain Haines had offered the stowaway, the faith received from Harry that should have kept Brian from temptation? Her own attempts to help him deepen his belief in God? She took little comfort in the fact his involvement with the Indian girl might well have been before she and Alice arrived. Harry's constancy to Alice rose to point up the difference between the two whose friendship must surely suffer with this new revelation. Her own position felt untenable. How could she face Brian O'Rourke now that she saw clearly what he really was? If only she could get away, go somewhere so far off she need never see him so long as she lived. She couldn't. A memory from weeks ago smote her. Her own voice accusing Alice, *"O ye of little faith."* She angrily dashed away the memory. The two situations bore no resemblance whatsoever.

Heather didn't realize how quickly the afternoon had waned until the familiar sound of hoofbeats and cheery greetings called from across the clearing announced the men's arrival and sent Alice flying to the doorway. Heather's lips curled in an unpleasant line and she turned to the badly neglected task of preparing supper. It would be a freezing day in August before Brian O'Rourke received any indication of further friendship from her.

Yet a sob rose to her throat when she thought of Crying Dove at the O'Rourke Palace, waiting. . . waiting.

eleven

When Brian failed to come to the Templeton cabin for supper, Alice told Harry in the fewest possible words of Crying Dove's presence at the Blarney Castle and the reason why.

Face fiery red, he leaped from his chair. His hazel eyes flashed with righteous indignation. "And you dare to believe such a thing?" he thundered, turning his gaze first to Alice, then to Heather. "How could you, after knowing him all this time."

A spurt of hope flared in his twin's traitorous heart. Harry plunged out the door with a, "Just wait until I get back," called over his shoulder.

"I-I've never seen him so angry," Alice quavered.

"Nor I." Heather stared out the open doorway. A little peace from the familiar clearing bordered with trees sank into her heart.

Hours later, Harry returned. He walked like an old man, yet faith that knew no bounds remained in his dulled eyes.

"Well?" Alice's whisper sounded loud in the stillness.

"We'll say no more about it but I believe a grave injustice is being done." Harry's lips twisted. He slumped into a chair by the table and poked down a little of the supper Alice had kept warm.

"What did he say?" Heather had to know.

"Just that Crying Dove will remain in the Blarney Castle. He's moving to the bunkhouse tonight."

"It's a little late, isn't it?" Could that hateful, condemning voice be *hers*? Heather would have given anything to recall the words.

"*Be still*. You know nothing of this." Harry's cup crashed to the table.

It cut her to the heart. Never had he spoken so. She felt an invisible wall rise between them, a barrier even twinship could not scale or shatter. Without a word, she rose and went to her room.

Just before she closed her door, she heard Alice plead, "Don't be too hard on her. I believe she cares for Brian."

Harry's tones stayed unforgiving. "Even more reason to have a little trust in him. No one else will, but God and me." His harsh laugh grated on the listening girl's nerves like a saw hitting a gnarled knot. "Living in the bunkhouse is going to be hellish. I asked him to come here but he flatly refused. If what you say is true, it's probably because of Heather." A little silence followed, then he added, "Alice, even if all the evidence were to the contrary would you keep on trusting—supposing I stood in Blarney's place?"

"Nothing on earth could make me believe evil of you."

Heather closed the door, heart aching. Why couldn't she be strong like Alice, whose instant reply proclaimed her far above the doubting Thomas who leaned against her bedroom door for support? Could it be an awful mistake? If so, would Brian ever forgive her? She stumbled to her bed and fell to her knees, wordlessly seeking God and asking for help she so sorely needed.

A few hours earlier, Brian's happy whistle died when he and Harry reached the clearing and only Alice appeared in the doorway. Although he always cleaned up and came back for the evening meal, just the daily glimpse of Heather smiling and waving to him erased the memory of a hard day's toil. His tune grew doleful, then cheerful again. Soon he would lay "heart, hand and worldly possessions" at his lady's feet. He grinned, a white streak in his bronzed face. Where had he picked up that gem of rhetoric? In any event, once he got the other business settled he would speak. A new softness in his object of adoration's manner since the cougar attack had raised his hopes. He daydreamed his way to the O'Rourke Palace, cared for his horse, and headed for the cabin. Another grin spread wide. The partly open door meant Heather and Alice had been there; sometimes they failed to latch the door properly.

Kicking off his cork boots outside the door and setting them neatly on the porch, he stockingfooted his way inside, expecting the aroma of fresh cookies or the scent of a wildflower bouquet. Neither greeted him.

"Why, Crying Dove!" He stopped just inside the cabin.

Defenseless, tragic, she waited, dark head bowed and hands gripped in her lap.

"What are you doing here?" He shook his head to clear it, knowing the answer before it came, the same answer that had shaken him weeks earlier and sent him pelting to Seattle on a fruitless errand.

"I have no other place." She looked up at him with eyes that held no hope, dark pools of misery.

Brian dropped heavily to a chair. So it had come, the time he dreaded. "Running Wolf—"

"No longer has a daughter." Her lips quivered and a silver bead slipped from one eye. "You said you would help me."

"I will," he repeated his vow. "First, I must think." His thoughts tumbled and formed solutions, none of them either acceptable or reasonable. Long before he decided anything other than the need to keep her at the cabin and remove to the logging camp bunkhouse, Harry Templeton burst in.

"What's all this nonsense?" he demanded.

Amidst the turmoil of uncertainty and hopelessness, his friend's ringing question and head held high poured into Brian's heart like oil into an open wound. Not a shred of doubt showed in the clear eyes, just pain on behalf of the other.

"Dove will be staying here," the accused managed to get out from behind the stump-sized obstruction in his throat. "I'll go to camp." He smiled at the girl, saw her tremulous smile, and herded Harry outside. "We'll be for needing to talk."

A long time later he spread his hands wide. "What else can I do?" he asked. "She must not be made to bear the blame."

"I don't know." Harry's shoulders slumped and he stared at the darkening sky. "But—marry her?"

"It may come to that."

"You'll have a hard time finding a white preacher to perform the ceremony," the younger man reminded.

"Maybe, though, under the circumstances. . ." His voice trailed off. "One thing, Blarney, promise me you won't go through with this until you have thought it over and weighed the results. Or until you have sought God with all your heart, as I will be doing."

"God?" Brian's mouth set in a white line. "What has He to do with it?" He caught back bitter words, knowing the futility of railing against life when it swept in ocean waves, claiming innocent victims as well as those black with sin.

"Give Him a chance. I believe in you, so does He." Harry's conviction made the words a benediction that lingered even when he left. All the way to the logging camp, Brian thought of them. They supported him through his stumbling explanation to the straw boss that he'd be bunking at camp at least for a few months. Too proud to lie or delay the storm he knew lay waiting to break over his head, he squared his shoulders, looked his boss in the eye, and quietly said, "Crying Dove is with child and needs a place to stay."

"Is there anything else you want to tell me?" A keen gaze bored into him and Brian wondered, but merely shook his head.

"It's not going to be easy for you. Some of the men have long admired the girl from a distance. Don't take too much guff," the straw boss warned.

"There's not much else I can be for doing, is there, sir?" Brian marched out before the man could reply. Yet every veiled reference to "men who fancy chocolate drops" and the open sneers by the worst elements in camp, who made no secret of their activities in Seattle, sent iron into Brian's soul. It took all his control not to rely on fists to shut mouths.

"It's 'cause you acted different," Miller frankly told him, then went on to punch a couple of heads when things got unbearable. No matter what the big logger personally felt, he loyally stayed friendly and on several occasions was heard to remark that fellers should be careful about pointing fingers; they always came back.

Brian hesitated about attending church the first Sunday. He knew news of Crying Dove's presence in his cabin had run rampant. How would he be treated? His heart pounded. One look into Heather Templeton's beautiful eyes would show what he both longed and dreaded to know. Yet the knowledge escaped him until after the preaching ended, leaving listeners stunned. With his usual boyish determination to tackle a problem head on, Harry chose valor rather than discretion and instead of simply giving a talk, preached with all the conviction of his young heart. His subject: "Let him that is without sin cast the first stone."

Brian felt he died a thousand deaths during the service, yet even through his misery he felt how the congregation that had congealed when he entered lost some of its hostility. Several regular members made a point to speak with him afterwards while others scuttled out to horses and buggies.

"Good morning, Mr. O'Rourke." The swish of skirts behind him spun Brian around. Alice stood smiling, round blue eyes compassionate, one lace-mitted hand extended. He briefly pressed it but couldn't help glancing over her shoulder to the brown-haired, yellow-clad figure behind her.

"Miss Heather?" He looked deep into her eyes. Hopes and dreams died. He saw a flicker that betrayed doubt, if not condemnation, mixed with a look of appeal that rocked him.

"Mr. O'Rourke." Her lifeless greeting confirmed what he read in her gaze and sent him out of the church as soon as he could leave without seeming discourteous. Harry's clarion halted him, left foot in the stirrup before mounting his waiting horse. "Come for Sunday dinner?"

"No, thank you." Brian swung into the saddle and kept his face averted. "I appreciate what you tried to do."

"Look, Blarney, I don't know how or when this is going to be settled but don't make it harder on your friends than it already is."

He glanced down into Harry's face. "You can't be for knowing what your faith means." He touched his horse's flanks with his heels and rode away without looking back. Behind lay everything he desired. Ahead lay duty and he knew a hundred fightings with self and others loomed large on his future's horizon. A flinty look dimmed the blue of his eyes. No use putting off what had to be done. He turned toward the only home he'd known since being sent away in Ireland. Thoughts churned and the steady beat of hooves covered the distance until he reined in at the Blarney Castle. Now that Heather was lost to him forever, the cabin didn't deserve the O'Rourke Palace designation.

Brian ran into a rock cliff when he outlined his plan to Crying Dove a little later. "It's the only thing to do," he told her. "The baby has to have a father."

She stubbornly shook her head. All his pleadings proved to be in vain. She would not agree to marry him. A lightning glance from her black eyes accompanied the refusal. "You do not love Crying Dove." Try as he would to convince her they had no other way open, she stayed firm and repeated again and again, "I cannot."

Brian finally gave up for the time being and headed back to the bunkhouse. A whiff from the distant Sound sent a thrust of longing into him. Why not follow its salty lure? He'd tried to do what he could for the Indian girl, to no avail. Perhaps the feel of a swaying deck beneath his feet, the sights and sounds and smells of foreign ports, the Southern Cross and strange languages and customs would in time dim the memory of a hazel-eyed lad who loved and trusted him, the twin sister who did not.

The next few days he alternated between arguing with Crying Dove and letting the seed planted by a strong west wind grow. If he sailed away, he could leave behind most of the hoard of earnings and inheritance from Captain Haines not used in building. Crying Dove's child would not be in need. She could remain in the Blarney Castle; surely Harry and Alice wouldn't mind. He refused to consider Heather's response to the new neighbor. Or if the child were a boy, Running Wolf might welcome his daughter back for the sake of a grandson, even one half-white.

Day after day, night after night, he worked and thought and felt the heart of him being torn. Leaving Washington Territory meant leaving the place that most resembled Ireland, with its greenness. Brian felt a little sick at the idea he might never see Mount Rainier again, the mountain the Indians called the *Mountain that was God*, a touching, if inaccurate name. The God he knew had never been a mountain but the Creator of them and the Father who loved erring children enough to send His Son to offer them salvation. Despite his earlier bitterness, the coming of Crying Dove had made Brian realize anew the extent of the sacrifice wherein One took the punishment on behalf of others. In a quiet glade one early September evening, the Irishman poured his heart out to God, asked for guidance and forgiveness, and rose with the light of purpose in his soul. Whether he stayed or went, Jesus Christ now reigned as Captain of his life.

&

All the joy of living in the wilderness had gone out like a snuffed candle for Heather. At times, she clung to Harry's unswerving faith in his friend, likening it to the wonderful words of James 1:5 and 6. *If any of you lack wisdom, let him ask of God, that giveth to all men liberally, and upbraideth not; and it shall be given him. But let him ask in faith, nothing wavering. For he that wavereth is like a wave of the sea driven with the wind and tossed.* At other times, the wealth of irrefutable evidence left her driven and tossed in spite of her prayers for wisdom. She grew thin, haunted by the sadness she had seen in Brian O'Rourke's Irish eyes. A long time ago, in what felt like another lifetime, she'd seen the same look in the eyes of a stray kitten she annexed and took home only to have Adelaide pick it up by the scruff of the neck and throw it into the street. She could only describe it as one who came to her for bread and received a stone.

Longing to do penance for her inability to give that which she could not control, Heather gladly joined Alice in her efforts to welcome Crying Dove. Blunt and practical as ever, Alice had said, "We used to hear in church about the need to take the gospel to the heathen. If we turn aside from her now, we're a pretty poor sort." So Heather helped knit and stitch and embroider. The new baby would lack for nothing in the way of clothing and blankets.

The Indian girl, who carried her child easily, bloomed from their loving care. She lost some of the hunted look and her slim face and body rounded. Yet now and then Heather saw an expression of resignation in her eyes. She'd said her baby would be born in early winter and for a few moments, the natural anticipation of the eternal mother love overshadowed her sadness. A natural dignity prevented the asking of questions and the three young women never discussed Brian or anything that had gone before Crying Dove's coming to the Blarney Castle. Once she stated simply, "O'Rourke is a good man," but didn't explain what she meant.

Heather went from stages of anger and shock through a kind of jealousy she despised in herself, to genuine concern and a tenuous love for the mother-to-be. Sometimes she compared her own feelings of leaving home and being in a strange land far from family with Crying Dove's situation. The difference left her ashamed. She'd had Alice, then Harry—and Brian. Crying Dove was dependent on strangers for succor and friendship.

A dozen, then a hundred times Heather reread James 1:5 and 6, until she decided on a bold stroke. She could

not as a child of God go on with a cluttered heart. Why
not ask for wisdom and follow what came as an answer? She began praying, not to know some mysteri-
ous truth but to forgive if it were needed and to replace
her accusations with faith, should it be justified. No
heavenly finger wrote across the autumn sky. No voice
spoke through the thunder. Yet as leaves fell, so did
the shackles that bound her. Early one morning when
frost lay thick as snow on the ground and the world
glistened with purity, Heather awakened to sunbeams
making rainbows on her white-clad window. Peace
pervaded every fiber of her being. She knew without
knowing how she knew, that Brian O'Rourke stood
guiltless of the sins heaped at his feet.

On fire with the eagerness to tell him, she hunted
and found writing materials, snatched up her Bible and
crawled back into bed. It took some time but at last
she jotted in a clear script the single reference, Job
33:9. The smile on her lips seeped into her heart. Yet
when she handed it to Harry before he left for work,
she simply said, "Here's a scripture for Brian."

Alice's mouth dropped open. Harry cocked an eyebrow but didn't say a word. Heather fled to the sanctuary of her room, wondering if Brian would think her
unmaidenly and wishing the day over so she could find
out.

⚬

Brian did not receive her message. Instead, he had a
visitor—unannounced and unexpected. A tall man with
anguish in his face appeared in the cook shack doorway while the loggers stowed away their enormous
breakfasts. Pale, hands trembling, he made an unsteady

way between tables until he reached Brian.

"Well, by the Great Horn Spoon, if it ain't the parson!" Miller leaped up grinning but Reverend Clifton ignored him.

"Your message just caught up with me," the minister said brokenly. Silence descended on the room. Jaws hung slack.

"Then you were for coming back on your own."

Dull red suffused the white skin. "Yes. I always meant to, but couldn't leave Mother when she was so ill. I took passage on the first ship after the funeral. Dear God, can you ever forgive me?"

Brian had the feeling that cry had wrenched itself from a tormented soul. "'Tis not my pardon you need to be asking."

"Hey, what's going on here?" Miller crossed his arms over his powerful chest and scowled. "We gotta finish eating and get to work. No time for all this jawin'."

The reverend threw back his head and faced the burly crew. "It's far past time, Miller." He closed his eyes, swallowed convulsively, and reopened them. "My wife, Crying Dove, is with child. I didn't know until I reached Seattle and got the letter O'Rourke sent months ago."

"*You*?" Miller gasped.

"*Wife*? Brian sprang to his feet, heart thudding.

"Of course. You didn't think—" Clifton's face turned to parchment. "Didn't she tell you?"

"No." The uncompromising syllable cut the stillness. "All she did was say she couldn't marry me, even for the child's sake."

Clifton tottered and would have fallen if Miller hadn't

grabbed him. "Then, everyone here thinks you. . ." He couldn't finish.

Miller shook him. "Blarney's been called everything under the sun on account of you." His face blackened. "Of all the lowdown, sneaking—"

"Stop, Miller. It's all over." Brian stared at the shaking preacher. "Before God, are you telling the truth?"

"Yes, by all that's holy. I fell in love with her the first time she walked into my church. I visited the village and she learned to care." He wrenched free and stood taller and straighter than anyone there had ever seen him. "Men, I knew what the world would say but didn't care. We became man and wife in an Indian ceremony to be followed by a minister's blessing, if I could find a man to give it. I honored Crying Dove and still do. Mother left enough for us to go away with our child." Unashamed tears came to his eyes. "Brian, I'm sorry."

The Irishman had to adjust his thinking. All these weeks and months Crying Dove had kept back the fact her baby was conceived in wedlock. Why? He asked Clifton.

"Running Wolf married us privately and agreed to keep it secret until I returned."

"Then threw her out when he discovered she would have a baby." Brian shook his head. How little he understood a culture so different from his own! Stay, was it? He remembered the persecution he'd experienced in the last weeks. An Indian maiden obviously deserted by a white man but carrying his child brought shame on a chief.

"Where is she?"

"At the O'Rourke Palace." Brian headed toward the door. "Boys, tell the boss I won't be for working today. It's my guess he'll rant and rave and then grin when he finds out why."

Clifton no longer rode a sorry nag but a good horse. He and Brian took a shortcut toward the cabin in the bigger clearing and missed Harry, on his way to work. "Before I take you to Crying Dove, you're to tell the story again," Brian told his companion. "You're for owing me that."

"Gladly. If I had dreamed what lay ahead, somehow I'd have managed to take Crying Dove with me," the reverend said. Regret lingered in his words, both then and when he confessed the secret marriage to Alice and a white-faced Heather. After the first glance, Brian didn't look at her again, yet the memory of enormous eyes remained with him.

"I just wanted you to know," he said quietly and stepped outside.

"Brian, wait!" The patter of feet announced Heather.

He half-turned. Now that he'd been exonerated, she would apologize, he thought bitterly. Why, oh why, hadn't she trusted him when he needed it most, no matter how black things seemed? "Yes?" His gaze lingered on her upturned face, lovely even with its troubled expression.

"Does Harry know? Did you see him this morning?" She seized his arm with shaking fingers.

"The boys will have told him but I've not seen him." His hurt over her doubts made him speak curtly.

"Oh!" She pulled away, face stricken. "Brian, you— I— there's so much to say. I am so sorry."

Numb rather than elated, although he felt the weight of the world had been lifted from his back, Brian shook his head. "There's nothing to say." He remounted his horse. "Reverend, I'd best go with you, if you don't mind." Leaving Heather standing near the prickly bush from which she took her name, he rode away, wondering how he could have once thought she'd bloom at the O'Rourke Palace, along with a start of the carefully transplanted sprigs.

"Let me go in alone," Clifton begged when they reached the cabin. Brian considered, then nodded. Joy never killed anyone and Crying Dove would be no exception. He waited until he heard the sound of weeping that followed the reverend's entrance to the cabin, then turned away. The need for solitude sent him deep into the forest. Later he must go see Running Wolf and reason with him. His own future lay blighted. Even if what he had seen in Heather Templeton's face reflected love, how could they be happy together? Wouldn't her failure always be between them? Yet as the day wore on, he felt on the brink of a great truth and at last it came, after earnest prayer. He must forgive her, as he had been forgiven. Yes, she had failed to live up to his hopes. Hadn't he failed a hundred times to live up to God's dreams? God didn't allow his falling short to stand between them.

Renewed and penitent, he whispered, "Thank You" but could say no more. He resented the time it took to get back to the Templeton cabin and leaped from his horse before it slid to a stop. "Heather?" He ran toward the porch to be met by a hazel-eyed whirlwind.

"Oh, Harry! Where's your sister?"

"Praise be!" Harry embraced him with a mighty grip. "I knew you were innocent."

"Yes, and your faith in me is what kept me from sinking," Brian told him. "Where's Heather? I've spent the day in the woods and have been for learning some things. About forgiveness."

"I'm glad." Harry released his friend and made a low bow. "I believe you'll find her inside."

"Not yet," Alice said from the doorway. "Harry Templeton, did you give Brian the message Heather sent to him this morning?"

"This morning?"

Brian looked at the other man who sheepishly fumbled in his pocket and muttered, "You'd hightailed it off before I got to work and I plumb forgot it."

"It doesn't matter." Brian felt impatience sweep through him. "Send Heather out, will you, please?"

Alice's round face set in obstinate lines. "She says you have to read the message before she will see you." She pulled a small Bible from her capacious apron pocket. "She said you will need this."

"Women!" Harry looked skyward, then held out a hand to Alice. "Let's go see how the garden's growing." Alice grinned and tripped down the steps. Her head bobbed alongside her husband's shoulder and their voices dwindled.

Wondering at Heather's strange actions, Brian unfolded the scrap of paper and read, "Job 33:9." He opened the Bible and turned pages. When he came to the right place, he stood riveted to the ground.

I am clean without transgression, I am innocent; neither is there iniquity in me.

He read it again and recalled Alice's words, ". . .the message Heather sent. . .this morning." A cry of gladness poured from his throat. The single scripture that meant so much had been written before he brought Reverend Clifton to tell his story and clear Brian O'Rourke's name. All the while he'd struggled in the forest, the message had lain in Harry's pocket. The wonder of it all struck Brian dumb.

A white figure appeared in the doorway. Questioning hazel eyes looked into Irish blue ones, then Heather sprang forward into Brian's open arms.

And by their feet, the heather bush that had survived so many trials along with them, brightened the clearing with its purple-rose, bell-shaped blossoms to be remembered even when winter snows came and hid its beauty until time for it to bloom once more.

To readers of *Flower of Seattle*

❧

There's more—about Brian and Heather, Harry and Alice, their families and friends—coming soon in *Flower of the West*. The book also introduces lovable but capricious Daisy Templeton O'Rourke who possesses her mother's charm and father's love of wandering; cowboy John Talbot; and the exciting life led by the Harvey Girl waitresses in the northern Arizona of the early 1900s.

A Letter To Our Readers

Dear Reader:

In order that we might better contribute to your reading enjoyment, we would appreciate your taking a few minutes to respond to the following questions. When completed, please return to the following:

Rebecca Germany, Editor
Heartsong Presents
P.O. Box 719
Uhrichsville, Ohio 44683

1. Did you enjoy reading *Flower of Seattle*?
   ❑ Very much. I would like to see more books
      by this author!
   ❑ Moderately
      I would have enjoyed it more if _____

   _____

2. Are you a member of *Heartsong Presents*? Yes   No
   If no, where did you purchase this book? _____

   _____

3. What influenced your decision to purchase this book? (Check those that apply.)

   ❑ Cover   ❑ Back cover copy

   ❑ Title   ❑ Friends

   ❑ Publicity   ❑ Other _____

4. On a scale from 1 (poor) to 10 (superior), please rate the following elements.

    ___Heroine   ___Plot

    ___Hero   ___Inspirational theme

    ___Setting   ___Secondary characters

5. What settings would you like to see covered in *Heartsong Presents* books?

_____

_____

6. What are some inspirational themes you would like to see treated in future books?_____

_____

_____

7. Would you be interested in reading other *Heartsong Presents* titles?   ❏ Yes   ❏ No

8. Please check your age range:
❏ Under 18   ❏ 18-24   ❏ 25-34
❏ 35-45   ❏ 46-55   ❏ Over 55

9. How many hours per week do you read? _____

Name _____

Occupation _____

Address _____

City _____ State _____ Zip _____

VeraLee Wiggins

The Forerunners

···· Hearts ♥ng ····

...... Presents ......

```
__HP56  A LIGHT IN THE WINDOW, Janelle Jamison
__HP59  EYES OF THE HEART, Maryn Langer
__HP60  MORE THAN CONQUERORS, Kay Cornelius
__HP63  THE WILLING HEART, Janelle Jamison
__HP64  CROWS'-NESTS AND MIRRORS, Colleen L. Reece
__HP67  DAKOTA DUSK, Lauraine Snelling
__HP68  RIVERS RUSHING TO THE SEA, Jacquelyn Cook
__HP71  DESTINY'S ROAD, Janelle Jamison
__HP72  SONG OF CAPTIVITY, Linda Herring
__HP75  MUSIC IN THE MOUNTAINS, Colleen L. Reece
__HP76  HEARTBREAK TRAIL, VeraLee Wiggins
__HP79  AN UNWILLING WARRIOR, Andrea Shaar
__HP80  PROPER INTENTIONS, Dianne Christner
__HP83  MARTHA MY OWN, VeraLee Wiggins
__HP84  HEART'S DESIRE, Paige Winship Dooly
__HP87  SIGN OF THE BOW, Kay Cornelius
__HP88  BEYOND TODAY, Janelle Jamison
__HP91  SIGN OF THE EAGLE, Kay Cornelius
__HP92  ABRAM MY LOVE, VeraLee Wiggins
__HP95  SIGN OF THE DOVE, Kay Cornelius
__HP96  FLOWER OF SEATTLE, Colleen L. Reece
```

Great Inspirational Romance at a Great Price!

Heartsong Presents books are inspirational romances in contemporary and historical settings, designed to give you an enjoyable, spirit-lifting reading experience. You can choose from 96 wonderfully written titles from some of today's best authors like Colleen L. Reece, Brenda Bancroft, Janelle Jamison, and many others.

When ordering quantities less than twelve, above titles are $2.95 each.

SEND TO: Heartsong Presents Reader's Service
P.O. Box 719, Uhrichsville, Ohio 44683

Please send me the items checked above. I am enclosing $_____.
(please add $1.00 to cover postage per order. OH add 6.25% tax. NJ add 6%.). Send check or money order, no cash or C.O.D.s, please.
To place a credit card order, call 1-800-847-8270.

NAME _____

ADDRESS _____

CITY/STATE_____ ZIP _____

LOVE A GREAT LOVE STORY?
Introducing Heartsong Presents —
                    Your Inspirational Book Club

Heartsong Presents Christian romance reader's service will provide you with four never before published romance titles every month! In fact, your books will be mailed to you at the same time advance copies are sent to book reviewers. You'll preview each of these new and unabridged books before they are released to the general public.

These books are filled with the kind of stories you have been longing for—stories of courtship, chivalry, honor, and virtue. Strong characters and riveting plot lines will make you want to read on and on. Romance is not dead, and each of these romantic tales will remind you that Christian faith is still the vital ingredient in an intimate relationship filled with true love and honest devotion.

Sign up today to receive your first set. Send no money now. We'll bill you only $9.97 post-paid with your shipment. Then every month you'll automatically receive the latest four "hot off the press" titles for the same low post-paid price of $9.97. That's a savings of 50% off the $4.95 cover price. When you consider the exaggerated shipping charges of other book clubs, your savings are even greater!

THERE IS NO RISK—you may cancel at any time without obligation. And if you aren't completely satisfied with any selection, return it for an immediate refund.

TO JOIN, just complete the coupon below, mail it today, and get ready for hours of wholesome entertainment.

Now you can curl up, relax, and enjoy some great reading full of the warmhearted spirit of romance.